SARA MAITLAND

On Becoming a Fairy Godmother

OTHER FICTION BY SARA MAITLAND

Daughter of Jerusalem

Telling Tales

Virgin Territory

A Book of Spells

Arkytypes
(with Michelene Wandor)

Three Times Table

Women Fly when Men aren't Watching

Home Truths

Brittle Joys

SARA MAITLAND

On Becoming a Fairy Godmother

Published in 2003 by
The Maia Press Limited
82 Forest Road
London E8 3BH
www.maiapress.com

Versions of 'Loving Oedipus' and 'Maid Marion's Story'
were broadcast by BBC Radio 4 in 2001 and 2002

ISBN 1 9045590 0 X

A CIP catalogue record for this book is available
from the British Library

Printed and bound in Great Britain by Thanet Press

'Time and trouble will tame an advanced
young woman, but an advanced old woman
is uncontrollable by any earthly force'
Dorothy Sayers

Contents

Why I Became a Plumber

~

One of the problems for the menopausal woman,
both medically and socially, is the relative silence
on flushing and similar symptoms
Pamphlet on the menopause (Boots the Chemist)

One of the advantages of the double trap
siphonic system, worth considering in some
locations, is its relative silence on flushing
Simple Plumbing (Cassells, 1989)

One of the easiest ways to distinguish the
Jack Snipe from the Common Snipe is its
relative silence on flushing
Pocket Guide to British Birds (Collins, 1966)

FOR MY SILVER WEDDING ANNIVERSARY my husband gave me a garden; a garden of rich loam, south facing, well planted in some distant past so that there were mature shrubs and fruit trees and a white mulberry in the centre; but a garden which had been more recently neglected so that there was lots of work to do and decisions to make. And, because gardens tend to come that way, this garden had a house attached to it – a dear little house built of mellow brick which, on sunny days, seemed to absorb heat and radiance through the day and then, in the evening, give it off again so that the house glowed warm after the sun had set.

I was delighted. It was the best present anyone could be given. I thought my husband had bought it as a retirement home. In a sense this was true. What I had failed to grasp was that it was *my* retirement home, not ours. That after twenty-five years on the job of wife I had been rendered redundant. The garden, and the house with it, was not a silver wedding present, but a golden handshake. The firm had engaged a new, bright young thing, who would do all my work and then some. I think I might have been able to bear it better if she had been some bimbo. I could then think of my husband as a naughty child, greedily meeting his desires as a child does. She was not. She was actually quite like me, but fifteen years younger. She loved him, and was sorry that all this had to happen to me. Quite likely it was she who insisted on my handsome pay-off.

I'm fairly certain though that it was not she who insisted on the way he chose to tell me. The first night in the new house we had sex and he made love with an exuberant energy – a renewal of a somewhat neglected interest – and then while my ribs still felt the weight of his presence, he informed me that this was the last time. I honestly think that he thought that if he gave me a really good rogering it would last me a nice long time and he would not have to feel guilty. Men, as no doubt you have noticed, are rather inclined to overestimate their own sexual performance. Given they are honest – though misled – about this, would you say that it was a kindly and generous impulse on his part, or a final arrogant cruelty? I had been sacked – sacked and looted and pillaged; perhaps it was only proper that I should be raped as well.

Then he pushed off – no doubt feeling that he had scraped through the whole embarrassing thing rather smoothly and that I had always wanted a garden, so everyone was happy. But I was not happy. I was in shock. For about ten weeks I just huddled in a heap.

Then I had a miscarriage.

Although it was nearly eighteen months since my last period and I had given the matter no thought, I know a miscarriage when I have one – in fact, I'm a bit of an expert. I curled up in bed shaken by pain and waiting for the whole horrible thing to be over. Then I phoned for an ambulance and had them take me to the hospital for the tedious and nasty business of getting my poor weary womb scraped clean.

'Why don't we just take it all out for you?' they asked.

'No, thank you,' I said.

'Hormone replacement therapy is jolly good now, you know.'

'No, thank you,' I said.

I didn't tell my husband; I really felt that I could do without his guilt-driven sympathy just then.

They sent me home quite soon.

It was a few weeks after this that I began to hear the singing.

At first it was just odd notes, clear but off-hand, if you know what I mean. The sort of singing that you might get if a choirboy of considerable ability just happened to be singing to himself as he walked up the road outside my house.

The singing became more frequent and clearer and louder. There was nothing exactly scary about this because it was heart-wringingly beautiful music. On the other hand, if you are a woman of that certain age, who is just recovering from a distinctly female complaint and trying to get used to being dumped by her husband, even the most lovely music, welling up from an unknown source and filling your house with a joy you cannot share, is a bit disturbing. More disturbing, however, was the discovery – or rather the realisation – that the singing came from the loo. Peripatetic choirboys along rural byways are unexpected, but invisible choirboys in the downstairs lavatory are rather more than that.

Anyway, the singing, it transpired, did not come from the lavatory in general; it came quite specifically from the toilet bowl itself. It always stopped abruptly if I went in, but there would be a slight disturbance of the water – a quivering of ripples bouncing as though I had dropped a small stone into the pan. The music came up as solidly as the stone would go down.

I thought that perhaps my dead baby was crying for me. There was within the pure and lovely sound an unbearable sadness, a yearning, that called to me for love. The baby, I believed, wanted me as much as I wanted it. I tried to catch the singer out. I'd leap into the room the moment the music started, pouncing on the bowl. I'd leave the door ajar and try and sneak in on bended tiptoe. I even arranged a small net, hanging from the seat. Such techniques produced nothing, but I had to find out: quite apart from anything else, I was getting constipated as well as curious.

The long-wanted garden went undug. The kind letters from old friends asking me to spend the weekend with them, or inviting themselves to inspect my new home, went unanswered. I unplugged the phone so as not to disrupt my vigils in the hallway. I was consumed with longing and with concentration. I do not think I have worked so hard on anything since the day I finally realised and accepted that soufflé was, and forever would be, beyond my culinary capabilities.

Finally I tried something different. I went into the lavatory when it was silent. I crouched down beside the loo itself, but craftily – so that my head was not in the line of vision from anywhere near the water level. I waited. I waited through stiffness and discomfort, beyond cramp, long past boredom and way after sleepiness. And in the late afternoon, when a long yellow finger of sun angled itself through the window and, picking up every dancing dust mote on its way, just touched the surface of the water, I was rewarded. There was a gurgly noise, some frolicsome splashing, a gentle laugh, and then the singing started.

Quick as a thought I attacked. Swooping like a gannet on its prey, I plunged both hands down into the water, grabbing wildly but efficiently at what I knew had to be there. I felt a thrashing, a fighting, then a despairing wriggle and finally a sudden relaxation, a dead weight against my palms. Alarmed I drew them up and looked at what I had caught. Between the clenched fourth and fifth fingers of my left hand the end of a tail, moss green and scaled with silver edges, hung out. Where my thumbs and index fingers met there were strands of equally green, green thread. Without relaxing my attention for an instant, I struggled to my feet and took my trophy to the wash-basin, and there inspected my catch. In my hands I held a very small mermaid.

She had fainted dead away, her tiny eyelids, grey-shadowed, covered her eyes and her long green lashes lay against her milk-white cheeks. I was not sure what you did with a passed-out mermaid. I could not push her head between her knees, because of course she had no knees. I placed her, looking decidedly seedy, into my primrose yellow pedestal sink. I felt worried and guilty. I reached for the cold tap and allowed a few drips to fall on her. Under her tiny but wonderfully full breasts I could see her ribs flutter to the beat of her heart; so I knew she was not dead. I picked up my cologne and waved the bottle under her nose – or, more accurately given the scale of things, over her face.

Suddenly she sneezed, sat up abruptly and said, 'Oh, a midday curse on the double trap siphonic lavatory suite.'

Retrospectively I do not know what I thought a mermaid would say if she happened to recover from a shocking faint to find herself not only in a stupid pastel-coloured sink, but with an enormous, concerned face looming over her. Certainly not that.

I was startled into saying, 'What?'

'A double trap siphonic toilet arrangement. That's what you've got and that's what's to blame for all this.'

Then suddenly she grinned like a child, and said, 'Excuse me, that was rude; please remember I've never seen this end of you before, only the other end.' And when I gaped at her dimly, she giggled and added, 'It's a very nice bum actually; don't worry about it.'

She had brilliant green eyes, and this strange green hair and the tail and a stunning figure – which is quite a lot for someone so small to have all at once.

'Does it hurt if I touch you?' I asked.

'No,' she replied, 'it was the shock, not the pain that made me pass out.' So very gently, using only one finger, I stroked her head.

'That's nice,' she murmured. 'Could you put some more water in this pond, please?'

I turned the cold tap on and let it run until the sink was half full. She cavorted with pleasure, dancing and diving in the little waves. I thought, 'I'm going crazy.' Then I thought, 'So what? This is fun.'

When she felt comfortable she sat up, sort of bobbling on the water, and we looked at each other with open curiosity.

'Why did you grab me like that?' she asked, perhaps a little aggrieved.

'I just wanted to know what was going on; who was making the music,' I told her. Then I remembered that I had hoped it was my baby and quite without my meaning to I started to weep; not the wild angry tears of the weeks after he had left me, but sad sweet tears for the child I had lost and the body that had betrayed me. My tears splashed into the sink and the mermaid caught and drank them.

'Salt!' she cried, 'oh, sweet salt! And I thought I would never taste it again.'

This made me think, so I snuffled and sniffed a bit and asked, 'But why are you here? What are you doing in *my* loo?'

'I got stuck,' she said, almost shamefaced. 'It's all the fault of this new-fangled plumbing.'

Involuntarily I glanced at my loo: it was one of those low-slung modern numbers. I had given its technology no thought. Until that moment I had never, I am ashamed to say, given any loo much thought; unless it were blocked and then my husband, in a manly way, had rung the plumber, who had usually complained that I had been putting unsuitable objects down it, and he and my husband would exchange that 'poor dears' look. Even thinking about this brought on a hot flush. I stood there while blood pumped up from below my waist and sweat pumped down my back and I felt a sulky expression, half shame-filled, half defiant, take over my features and I wanted to cry some more.

'What a pretty colour!' exclaimed my little mermaid, 'I'm very fond of pinks, they're so opposite from greens.' I felt better immediately and returned to the business.

'So, what's wrong with my loo?'

'It's one of those double trap siphonic contraptions,' said the mermaid grumpily, 'I told you that already.'

'But I don't know what that means.'

'Well, you shouldn't have installed one then. From your point of view it means it takes up more space than the old-style works, but that is compensated for by its relative silence on flushing. And, of course, it uses less water which is important ecologically, but extremely unfortunate for me. From my point of view it means that I can't get back out into the mains water system – just like a salmon par when someone builds a dam.'

(I never did discover what she had been doing in the freshwater channels in the first place – she could be a little shy about personal matters, and I've always hated being cross-questioned myself.)

'Would you like something to eat?' I asked her – I could not imagine there was much nutrition in the sewage system.

'Thank you, but I don't eat,' she said politely, 'but could I have a comb and mirror, please? We are nourished by our own loveliness.' I noticed that as she said this her cheeks were suffused with the palest apple-green tinge – the mermaid equivalent of a blush, as I was to learn. It did make a lovely contrast with menopausal flush pink.

The mirror was easy, but a comb her size was hard. In the end I went into town and bought a Fashion-Barbie-Accessory-Selection.

'For your granddaughter, madam?' asked the smiling salesgirl.

'No, for my mermaid,' I said without thinking.

She gave me a distinctly fishy look. The day before I would have been embarrassed, but now I just giggled. This seemed to perturb her somewhat.

So, suddenly it was spring-time; a greener spring than I had ever known and sparkling with promise and delight. Fresh gold greens of dawn; soft sweet greens of noontide; luminous thick greens of evening; and rich dark greens of dreams. And none of them as green, as fresh, as sweet, as rich, as varied as the greens of her tail and her eyes. None as green as her laughter.

I bought her a fish bowl, since I could not spend all my time in the hall toilet. The round one we tried first proved most unsatisfactory; it distorted our views of each other. So I bought the larger rectangular kind, and then realised that it was exactly the same as the crib in the Intensive Care Unit where my long-ago baby had died, and I cried and I cried.

To comfort me she sang – and to her singing I wept all the tears of the long years away, and was genuinely happy to see my husband when he called by about the divorce settlement. This seemed to perturb him somewhat.

She and I talked – and talking to her I became open and fluent and quick as a green highland burn. I rang my old friends and chatted, buoyantly, wittily, happily. This seemed to perturb them somewhat.

And, being knowledgeable in such matters, she taught me plumbing.

By the end of June I was explaining politely to the man from the Water Board that I did know the difference between pressure and flow, so he did not need to patronise me. This seemed to perturb him somewhat.

In the middle of July I installed my own power-shower. (Bliss.)

And by August I had come to recognise how many women get and stay married because they are afraid of the plumber. I decided that that winter I would go on a car maintenance course and then I would not be afraid of anybody.

My mermaid checked that cars did not have dangerous slicing propellers and, once reassured, laughed and sang a high G so pure and glorious that the wine glasses reverberated, humming different notes in a perfect harmonic scale. To reward her for this stunt I took my engagement ring and had one of its emeralds taken out and made into a choker for her.

'What's it *for*?' asked the young jeweller, curious about mounting a single emerald (a very small one, we had been poor though optimistic then) on a fine gold chain less than two inches long.

'It's a necklace for my mermaid,' I said.

This seemed not to perturb him at all. He just smiled. When I went to collect the choker he had added two seed pearls, one either side of the emerald, and he did not charge for them. I laughed with pure joy. I might well be mad, but I was not alone in my madness and anyway it was fun.

I was so happy that summer.

It took me until September; until the horse chestnut trees were dark matt green, and their shiny nuts crashed from the branches and lay, cradled in silk, inside their split shells. It took me until the evenings were heavy green, until the green flash on the cock-pheasant's neck stood out in the cut cornfields. It took me until autumn to accept that the little mermaid was not as happy as I was.

At first I did not notice.

Then I tried not to notice.

Then I pretended not to notice.

One evening we had a thunderstorm; green flashes of lightning across the green evening sky. And afterwards the air was pure and soft and cool and she sang. She sang that night so sweetly that two dog foxes came to sit in the garden to hear her; and a moth dechrysalised eight months early and thought death a cheap price to pay for such music. There was within that pure and lovely sound an unbearable sadness, a yearning that called to me for love.

So I said, 'Do you want to go back to the sea?'

Deep within her green eyes was a flash of desire, come and gone like a moon-bow in the spray of a waterfall. I started to weep again as I had not wept since the spring.

'Not much,' she said, but her eau-de-Nil flush betrayed her.

I had her at my mercy. I wanted to be mean and greedy and selfish and cruel. I needed her. I had a right to what I needed. All I had to do was pretend to believe her.

'You're not a good liar,' I told her.

I picked up her intensive care container and carried it out to the car. There were still the remnants of thunder in the air, but the sky was clearing. The moon appeared all silver furbelowed from behind a silver cloud.

It was forty-eight miles to the nearest coast, and I could not even drive fast because of sloshing her about. A slow mile for each year of my slow life. Anyway I was crying all the time, which made driving particularly tricky.

When we reached the shore it was so late that it was early again, the dark paling enough to make a grey skyline far, far out to sea. There was a whispering, a murmuring of waves. I parked the car in some rough grass, as near to the pebble beach as I could go. I sat there for a long time and she watched me, silent now. There was the first movement of birds stirring out towards the end of the bay – duck probably, and higher, invisible, the drift of gulls. One of them cried out and I moved at last. I opened the car door and stretched. The stretching made me sneeze, and the sound of the sneeze flushed out a Jack Snipe couched in a tussock almost at my feet. It was still too dark to see that snakeskin pattern on its back, but I knew it by the fierce draught of its wings and its zigzag, silent departure. I cried out in shock and delight, and then turned and lifted the transparent tank from the passenger seat.

She just stared at me. I carried her down to the water's edge. The tide was full so it was not far enough. I lifted her out and held her for a moment.

She stretched up to her neck and I did not immediately understand what she was doing: she was trying to take off her necklace.

'No, keep it,' I said.

'Every time you flush your double trap siphonic toilet,' she told, 'in its relative silence you will hear me singing.' I saw her green tears welling.

She reached up a tiny finger and touched my face.

I lowered my hands into the almost still water. It was shockingly cold. I don't have to do this, I thought. She can't make me. I'm bigger than her.

There was a frantic, powerful wriggle against my fingers and she was gone.

The pre-dawn air was suddenly bitter chill. I shivered. I could not see for tears and for my shaking. I turned away, stumbling on the shingle, groping for the hankie I never manage to have when I need it. Something made me turn back. Out there, in the free water, beyond the beach, I could see her. She was dancing in, on, with, the waves, lit by a green phosphorescence which had risen from the depths to welcome her home. Her tail was splashing joyfully. She was singing; I could hear her; she was singing a completely new song of freedom and joy. Within that pure and lovely sound there was no sadness, no yearning. She sang to me with love.

She looked towards the beach, saw me watching and threw up her pale arms – not drowning, but waving.

And that's why I became a plumber.

The Wicked Stepmother's Lament

~

THE WIFE OF A RICH MAN fell sick, and as she felt that her end was drawing near, she called her only daughter to her bedside and said, 'Dear child, be good and pious, and then the good God will always protect you, and I will look down from heaven and be near you.' Thereupon she closed her eyes and departed. Every day the maiden went out to her mother's grave and wept, and she remained pious and good. When winter came the snow spread a white sheet over the grave and by the time the spring sun had drawn it off again the man had taken another wife . . .

Now began a bad time for the poor step-child . . . They took her pretty clothes away, put an old grey bedgown on her and gave her wooden shoes . . . She had to do hard work from morning to night, get up before daybreak, carry water, light fires, cook and wash . . . In the evening when she had worked until she was weary she had no bed to go to but had to sleep by the hearth in the cinders. And as on that account she always looked dusty and dirty, they called her Cinderella.

You know the rest I expect. Almost everyone does.

I'm not exactly looking for self-justification. There's this thing going on at the moment where women tell all the old stories again and turn them inside-out and back-to-front – so the characters you always thought were the goodies turn out to be the baddies, and vice versa, and a whole lot of guilt is laid to rest: or that at least is the theory. I'm not sure myself that the guilt isn't just passed on to the next person, *in tacta*, so to speak. Certainly I want to carry and cope with my own guilt, because I want to carry and cope with my own virtue and I really don't see that you can have one without the other. Anyway, it would be hard to find a version of this story where I would come out a shiny new-style heroine: no true version, anyway. All I want to say is that it's more complicated, more complex, than it's told, and the reasons why it's told the way it is are complex too.

But I'm not willing to be a victim. I was not innocent, and I have grown out of innocence now and even out of wanting to be thought innocent. Living is a harsh business, as no one warned us when we were young and carefree under the apple bough, and I feel the weight of that ancient harshness and I want to embrace it, and not opt for some washed-out aseptic, hand-wringing, Disneyland garbage. (Though come to think of it he went none-too-easy on stepmothers, did he? Snow White's scared the socks off me the first time I saw the film – and partly of course because I recognised myself. But I digress.)

Look. It was like this. Or rather it was more like this, or parts of it were like this, or this is one part of it.

She was dead pretty in a Pears soap sort of way, and, honestly, terribly sweet and good. At first all I wanted her to do was concentrate. Concentration is the key to power. You have to concentrate on what is real. Concentration is not good or bad necessarily, but it is powerful. Enough power to change the world, that's all I wanted. (I was younger then, of course; but actually they're starving and killing whales and forests and each other out there; shutting your eyes and pretending they're not doesn't change anything. It does matter.) And what she was not was powerful. She wouldn't look out for herself. She was so sweet and so hopeful; so full of faith and forgiveness and love. You have to touch anger somewhere, rage even; you have to spit and roar and bite and scream and know it before you can be safe. And she never bloody would.

When I first married her father I thought she was so lovely, so good and so sad. And so like her mother. I knew her mother very well, you see; we grew up together. I loved her mother. Really. With so much hope and fondness and awareness of her worth. But – and I don't know how to explain this without sounding like an embittered old bitch, which I probably am – she was too good. Too giving. She gave herself away, indiscriminately. She didn't even give herself as a precious gift. She gave herself away as though she wasn't worth hanging on to. Generous to a fault, they said, when she was young, but no one acted as though it were a fault, so she never learned. 'Free with Kellogg's Corn Flakes' was her motto. She equated loving with suffering, I thought at one time, but that wasn't right, it was worse, she equated loving with being; as though she did not exist unless she was denying her existence. I mean, he was not a bad bloke, her husband, indeed I'm married to him myself, and I like him and we have good times together, but he wasn't worth it – no one is – not what she gave him, which was her whole self with no price tag on.

And it was just rhe same with that child. Yes, yes, one can understand: she had difficulty getting pregnant actually, she had difficulties carrying those babies to term too. Even I can guess how that might hurt. But her little girl was her great reward for suffering, and at the same time was also her handle on a whole new world of self-giving. And yes, of course she looked so lovely, who could have resisted her, propped up in her bed with that tiny lovely child sucking, sucking, sucking? The mother who denied her little one nothing, the good mother, the one we all longed for, pouring herself out into the child. Well, I'll tell you, I've done it too, it is hell caring for a tiny daughter, I know. Everything, everything drags you into hell: the fact that you love and desire her, the fact that she's so needy and vulnerable, the fact that she never leaves you alone until your dreams are smashed in little piles and shabby with neglect, the fact that pleasure and guilt come so precisely together, as so seldom happens, working towards the same end and sucking your very selfhood out of you. It is a perilous time for a woman, that nursing of a daughter, and you can only survive it if you cling to yourself with a fierce and passionate love, *and* you back that up with a trained and militant lust for justice *and* you scream at the people around you to meet your needs and desires *and* you do not let them off, *and* when all is said and done you sit back and laugh at yourself with a well-timed and not unmalicious irony. Well, she could not, of course she could not, so she did not survive. She was never angry, she never asked, she took resignation – that tragic so-called virtue – as a ninth-rate alternative to reality and never even realised she had been short-changed.

So when I first married my husband I only meant to tease her a little, to rile her, to make her fight back. I couldn't bear it, that she was so like her mother and would go the same way. My girls were more like me, less agreeable to have about the house, but tough as old boots and capable of getting what they needed and not worrying too much about what they wanted or oughted, so to speak. I didn't have to worry about them. I just could not believe the sweetness of that little girl and her wide-eyed belief that I would be happy and love her if she would just deny herself and follow me. So of course I exploited her a bit, pushed and tested it, if you understand, because I couldn't believe it. Then I just wanted her to *see*, to see that life is not all sweetness and light, that people are not automatically to be trusted, that fairy godmothers are unreliable and damned thin on the ground, and that even the most silvery of princes soon goes out hunting and fighting and drinking and whoring, and doesn't give one tuppenny-ha'penny curse more for you than you give for yourself. Well, she could have looked at her father and known. He hardly proved himself to be the great romantic lover of all time, even at an age when that would have been appropriate, never mind later. He had after all replaced darling

Mummy with me, and pretty damned quick too, and so long as he was getting his end off and his supper on the table he wasn't going to exert himself on her behalf, as I pointed out to her, by no means kindly.

(And, I should like to add, I still don't understand about that. I couldn't believe how little the bastard finally cared when it came to the point. Perhaps he was bored to tears by goodness, perhaps he was too lazy. He was a sentimental old fart about her, of course, his eyes could fill with nostalgic tears every time he looked at her and thought of her dead mother; but he never *did* anything; or even asked me to stop doing anything. She never asked, and he never had eyes to see, or energy or . . . God knows what went on in his head about her and as far as I'm concerned God's welcome. She loved him and trusted him and served him and he never even bloody noticed. Which sort of makes my point actually because he would never treat me like that, and yet he and I get on very well now; like each other and have good times in bed and out of it. Of course I'd never have let him tell me how to behave, but he might have tried, at least just once.)

Anyway, no, she would not see. She would not blame her father. She would not blame her mother, not even for dying, which is the ultimate outrage from someone you love. And she would not blame me. She just smiled and accepted, smiled and invented castles in the air to which someone, though never herself, would come and take her one day, smiled and loved me. No matter what I did to her, she just smiled.

So, yes, in the end I was cruel. I don't know how to explain it and I do not attempt to justify it. Her *wetness* infuriated me. I could not shake her good will, her hopefulness, her capacity to love and love and love such a pointless and even dangerous object. I could not make her hate me. Not even for a moment. I could not make her hate me. And I cannot explain what that frustration did to me. I hated her insane dog-like devotion where it was so undeserved. She treated me as her mother had treated him. I think I hated her stupidity most of all. I can hear myself almost blaming her for my belly-deep madness; I don't want to do that; I don't want to get into blaming the victim and she was my victim. I was older than her, and stronger than her, and had more power than her; and there was no excuse. No excuse, I thought the first time I ever hit her, but there was an excuse and it was my wild need, and it escalated.

So in the end – and yes I have examined all the motives and reasons why one woman should be cruel to another and I do not find them explanatory – so in the end I was cruel to her. I goaded and humiliated and pushed and bullied her. I used all my powers, my superior strength, my superior age, my superior intelligence, against her. I beat her, in the end, systematically and severely; but more than that I used her and worked her and denied her pleasures and gave her pain. I violated her space, her dignity, her integrity, her privacy, even her humanity and perhaps her physical safety. There was an insane urge in me, not simply to hurt her, but to have her admit that I had hurt her. I would lie awake at night appalled, and scald myself with contempt, with anger and with self-disgust, but I had only to see her in the morning for my temper to rise and I would start again, start again at her with an unreasonable savagery that seemed to upset me more than it upset her. Picking, picking and pecking, endlessly. She tried my patience as no one else had ever done and finally I gave up the struggle and threw it away and entered into the horrible game with all my considerable capacity for concentration.

And nothing worked. I could not make her angry. I could not make her hate me. I could not stop her loving me with a depth and a generosity and a forgivingness that were the final blow. Nothing moved her to more than a simper. Nothing penetrated the fantasies and daydreams with which her head was stuffed so full I'm surprised she didn't slur her consonants. She was locked into perpetual passivity and gratitude and love. Even when she was beaten she covered her bruises to protect me; even when she was hungry she would not take food from my cupboards to feed herself; even when I mocked her she smiled at me tenderly.

All I wanted was for her to grow up, to grow up and realise that life was not a bed of roses and that she had to take some responsibility for her own life, to take some action on her own behalf, instead of waiting and waiting and waiting for something or someone to come shining out of the dark and force safety on her as I forced pain. What Someone? Another like her father who had done nothing, nothing whatever, to help her and never would?

Another like him whom she could love generously and hopelessly and serve touchingly and givingly until weariness and pain killed her too. I couldn't understand it. Even when I beat her, even as I beat her, she loved me, she just loved and smiled and hoped and waited, daydreamed and nightdreamed, and waited and waited and waited. She was untouchable and infantile. I couldn't save her and I couldn't damage her. God knows, I tried.

And now of course it's just an ancient habit. It has lost its sharp edges, lost the passion in both of us to see it out in conflict, between dream and reality, between hope and cynicism. There is a great weariness in me, and I cannot summon up the fire of conviction. I do not concentrate any more, I do not have enough concentration, enough energy, enough power. Perhaps she has won, because she drained that out of me years and years ago. Sometimes I despair, which wastes still more concentration. We plod on together, because we always have. Sweetly she keeps at it, smile, smile, dream, hope, wait, love, forgive, smile, smile, bloody smile. Tiredly, I keep at it too: 'Sweep that grate.' 'Tidy your room.' 'Do your homework.' 'What can you see in that nerd?' 'Take out those damn earphones and pay attention.' 'Life doesn't come free, you have to work on it.' 'Wake up, hurry up, stop daydreaming, no you can't, yes you must, get a move on, don't be so stupid.' And 'You're not going to the ball, or party, or clubbing, or over your Nan's, dressed like *that*.'

She calls it nagging.

She calls me Mummy.

Witch-woman

~

Issobel Gowdie is gone for a witch.
weird witch woman and winter wind wailing
wise witch woman and wild wood wandering
Issobel Gowdie is gone for a witch
Issobel Gowdie of Auldearn in the county of Nairn.

1662 WAS A BAD YEAR. A long, raw winter. Cold. Damp. Long and cold and raw and damp, with the store crops rotting, iced to the core and growing grey-mauve down, webs of death laid on the food of life. The children from the hill clans came down to the river, begging, their pride broken by the cold and the bones of their cheeks standing high and fierce like dead warriors; their hands and their feet twisted, knurled, like old women.

Issobel Gowdie is gone for a witch

Far away in the south – as far away as story tales of the green queen under the hillside, in whom God has forbidden anyone to believe – there was a king again. The Black Boy come home, strutting and rutting on the city streets. Laughing in his triumph, but haunted by dreams of his father's head tumbling down, and the long years of patronage and contempt. Behind him, in secret rooms, by dim flickers and pacts with the devil, were the Jesuits, with thin white hands and slow dark plots. They were waiting, waiting. They had conjured the long dark winter and the edging hunger; they had nibbled down the margin of safety too thin, and they were biding their time.

Every Scot knew who had sold the old king to his death. The Scots had. The papists urged penance, the price of redemption, the blood price for the old king. The presbyters urged penance too, for the people had not proved deserving of their high calling, not worthy to be the new people of God, not worthy to build Zion here on the granite hills. In frivolity and in superstition, at bed and at table, by the highways and the backways, in the house and on the hillside, by land and by sea, they had sinned and God would smite them, and they would be damned. Damned. Damned. Damned by the vicious wind that blew in from the east across the grey sea. Damned to eternity.

weird witch woman and winter wind wailing

Those who have done well from the kingless years are frightened. Those whom the same years have treated less kindly are filled with a vengeful hope. The frail venturings out on to dangerous seas after herring runs and trading profits are fraught with nervous, greedy expectation. Young folk dream of the Americas, the new world; and old folk dream of death and decay, alone and untended.

wise witch woman and wild wood wandering

There is another rumour, a ground swelling. There is plague, plague coming hard on the heels of the hard winter. Hovering across the sea, lurking in every breath of the cold wind. Biding its time.

Issobel Gowdie is gone for a witch

King and weather. Plague and hunger. God and minister. Laird and beggar. Fear and ambition. None of these are the cause; they are just the froth thrown off by the evil at the core.

1662 was a bad year and it saw the climax of the witch-hunt. Over three hundred and ninety cases were brought to trial under the Witchcraft Act of 1593 in that bad year. More than one witch each day, every day, through cold winter and late spring and pallid summer and dank autumn.

Issobel Gowdie of Auldearn in the County of Nairn.
Issobel Gowdie is gone for a witch
Slutty, strutty Issobel Gowdie.

Not pretty. Never pretty – girl, woman or witch. That is the unforgivable thing. If you are a woman who struts herself down a village street so that every man – every man from twelve-year-old Thomas who raises a half-embarrassed finger to feel his upper lip and takes hope, right through to The Old One who looks up from his silent reverie and mumbles and cackles of what he did with Issobel Gowdie more than twenty years gone by . . . If you are a woman who walks the village street and every man, aye, even the newlyweds who can't keep their hands off their brides, and the old husbands who sleep snore-snorting and never turn to their faithful wives . . . If you are a woman whom every man watches, greedy and open with lust, then at the very least you should be pretty. Bad mistake, Issobel Gowdie, for you were never pretty, and yet, with every step of you, every turn of your head, the fire ignites, and they want you and know that they can have you and the women will never forgive you.

Issobel Gowdie is gone for a witch

If you can't be pretty, be young. If you are young, then somewhere there is a man, a man will come and tame you and reduce you to the ranks of the rest of us. If you are young, you can learn to be old; and what your man can't beat into you, your children will grind in. Be young and merry and kindly in your passing. It is a joke then, and we can wait you out, biding our time until your charms fade, until you are like we are. And then we can pity you, gossip about you and notice how little good ever comes of such ways, and warn our daughters by you.

Not young and not pretty and yet even the minister turns nervous pink and smiles as you pass and then frowns and snaps at the next innocent passer-by. You reek of straw mattress and cow byre, the sweet pungency of sex; and every man turns his head and dreams his dreams when you strut down the street; and we cannot tell why. You are too old for this and should have learned better; and you laugh too much and you show no shame, and we will never forgive you, Issobel Gowdie.

Issobel Gowdie is gone for a witch
and the moon blue silver with mauve clouds flying

Don't look to the men to protect you. Men protect what they own, what is theirs, and you are never theirs. They never possess you. They want and they yearn and their sweat drips over your breasts, so that when they finally get up to sneak home, there is a soft, sucking squelch as you separate, and then it is over. They have pleasured you, though they will never know whether more or less than the last man, and you have pleasured them. But they cannot fool themselves that they have taken you, known you, held you for one springing moment beyond your own choosing. They have not delved into your dreams, they do not crouch there with the power to make you weep or laugh. When you smile to yourself, they can never quite convince themselves that they caused the smile, the memory, the sweetness. They are sinners, lost in their own lusts, not hunters come home with their prey, warriors with their spoils. They will never forgive you.

It is shameful for a man to be wracked with desire for a woman he has known his whole lifetime; for a woman who dandled him as a baby and patted his childhood knees when he fell and whinged in the alley; for a woman whose hair ribbons he teased when he and she were young together; for a woman whose father had been his school mate. For a woman who is not pretty, nor young, nor needy; whose thighs have softened and whose hair looks dusty, not grey but faded. You have shamed them, Issobel Gowdie, and they will not forgive you.

Cold winter, distant plague, new hopes, old fears, religious disputes, political unease and a woman who walks out on to the village street and makes every man fidget.

You did not have a chance in that bad year, Issobel Gowdie.

Did you know what was coming?

There are murmurs. Below sound, secrets hidden in smiles, in charitable refusals, in soft sighs eliciting encouragement. Hoping for permission. Inviting intimacy. Exciting speculation. Mutters uttered. Children's questions silenced, then solicited. Little spits of gossip and guesswork. Each muted murmur, each whisper, winding a louder claim.

The night the ship went down – foundered senselessly on a still sea, under a full moon and five good men drowned – she was singing and laughing. They heard her in her house, singing and laughing on her own. They saw her on the street next morning scarlet red, like the devil, and sweat dripping from her, like a woman who had a hard night of it. But she had been alone. Singing and laughing. They had heard her. Singing and laughing.

I'm not one to gossip . . . no, really. But did you know . . . just between ourselves. You can trust me. I wouldn't tell a soul. She mentioned, I'm sure she meant no harm . . . he can't shake that cough; he spent all night and then the cough . . . They say the time the baby died . . . I've only heard. No, really. Please. Don't ask me, ask Moira. You know I'm not one for gossip . . . I could tell you a thing or three. Her time of life. Or longer. Always . . .

remember her mother . . . God forbid that I should . . . I didn't say, but since you ask . . .

Slut. Slut, whore.

But, my dear, how does she do it? At her age. *That* age.

Dangerous age. Dark passage for a woman.

Slut, whore, bitch

Then, suddenly, perhaps before anyone meant it, suddenly it has all gone too far.

Slut whore bitch. A pause. No one will ever know who says it first.

Slutwhorebitch. Witch.

Witch.

Witch.

Witch. Witch woman – wild, wise, weird, wind-wailing, wood wandering.

Issobel Gowdie is gone for a witch

So.

It is said, and there can be no going back.

Once the thing is named, it cannot be recalled. For if Issobel Gowdie is not a witch, then we are a mean, uncharitable and superstitious people. Cruel. Our men are randy dogs and our women foul-mouthed harridans. To say such a thing of a neighbour; a woman well known to us since childhood, a woman whose only fault is that she is neither young nor pretty and – God knows – in so long and cold a winter a woman must do what she can to warm heart and hearth. It is a hard time for a woman when her bairns are gone and her skin itches through the night and she must scratch, when her blood runs high in her face whether she will or no, when her body dreams itself through sweaty nights and cries out from old losses.

Witch. It is said. There can be no going back.

If we do not go back, then we must go forward. Somebody ought to do something. Arrest her. Send her before the Judge, to the Courts.

But the judges are heathen Southroners and may not understand. And who wants to go up to the great town and be a witness among people who do not know, who have not seen her strutting the street, who did not feel the horror of the lamb born twin-headed? People who may ask, not understanding, just how much Dutch rum the crew of the fishing smack had been drinking and whether the tax on it was ever paid? In the great town they may laugh at such country things; and we are all god-fearing simple folk who cannot work the long, wicked papish words around our honest tongues.

No. The Great Ones must take a hand. The Minister. The Laird. The Sheriff. The Session Clerk. This is what the gentry are for. The ones who can talk the sharp town talk, but know the sullen village silence.

They understand. They can be relied upon. They know the delicate balances of ill repute, malefice, surly rumours among the anxious and the expense of maintaining useless women on the parish. So they act. They send to Edinburgh for a licence to set up a Privy Council Commission for the trying and burning of Issobel Gowdie, witch.

Issobel Gowdie, of Auldearn in the county of Nairn, was brought for trial in May.

weird witch woman and winter wind wailing
wise witch woman and wild wood wandering

At first she hardly cares, she does not believe it, not any of it. It is ridiculous. A game from childhood.

They put her in the back shed of the Kirk, having no prison, and lock the door. She half giggles, for this is an old game, a game from childhood, that perhaps they are all too old to play, but boys will be boys, and girls do best to laugh merrily.

The witch searcher comes and sticks, or does not stick, pins in her back. Like children teasing, voices from forty years ago, words chanted in play that perhaps they are all too old to sing, but boys will be boys, and girls do best to laugh with them.

They do not let her sleep. Through the window of the shed they prod her with sticks each time her eyes close. This is very silly. It goes on too long, but fretted and weary she does not believe it, not any of it. It is a game from childhood, not the best game, but soon it will be evening and they will all go home laughing to warm soup and mother's spinning hands and the greening of the May night.

The Commission sends for her. She hears the key in the door, harsh in the morning, and she prepares a smile to show that forty years ago and still Issobel Gowdie is a bold lass who can take a rough joke. The prison warder does not meet her eyes, he will not meet her eyes, there is a mute shame in him, and in the dawn blur Issobel Gowdie feels the flicked whip of a cold wind against her legs.

It is a short walk. It is an old walk. She has walked down this village street a thousand times before.

It is the longest walk she has ever made. She has never, ever, been here before.

She sees her neighbours. The women stare boldly, unforgiving, eyes hard and faces closed. The men are half ashamed, they will not meet her glance, but look at their feet, unforgiving. Quite suddenly Issobel Gowdie is very afraid.

This is a new thing, this fear. For something went awry with Issobel Gowdie, right from a child. The prison wardens of girlhood whose silent feet pad, pad, pad through the dreams of girl children and of young women had failed to make her afraid. Pad, pad, pad they went all through the nights, but she had dreamed only of a moon, blue silver, with mauve clouds flying.

Every girl child must learn fear, and learn to call it virtue, so the world can be kept safe and well-ordered. But Issobel Gowdie's dreams were fierce and lovely and the pad, pad, pad of the silent feet never reached her in her sleep. So she knew no fear: not of reputation, nor of damnation, nor of loneliness, nor of cold, nor of old age, nor of lovelessness, nor of men, nor of God. Not having learned fear as a child, it could not grow on her as a grown woman, could not tame, constrain, maim or diminish her. Issobel Gowdie walked the street of Auldearn as a little child walks; believing that the world was a sweet place and full of joy, that life was a gift given, and risk was a sugar bun that raises laughter and wildness. No shadows.

She had been so for fifty years and now this flick of fear, this whipping coldness, this new hard fist in her lower belly made her not humble but angry. And anger made her laugh and laughter made her powerful.

'Well, Issobel Gowdie,' she whispers to herself, 'you've gone too far this time. You're gone for a witch.'

By the time she stepped into the hall where the Commissioners sat, nervous, self-important and waiting to exercise their authority, Issobel Gowdie knew that this was her last day. By nightfall they will have had her strangled with a thin cord and burned for a witch. There was no other way. She knew.

When it is like this, when you know what is coming, when you see clearly that there is no escape, no choice, no tiny corner in which to hide, then you are either terribly, terribly frightened or you are free. Issobel Gowdie had no practice in fear and was much accomplished in freedom. When they are out to get you, there may well come a time when femininity and innocence and sweetness itself won't serve. Then you have to dig deep into the resources of your own imagination and of all the stories you have ever heard and come out proud and wild and free. So she did. If she is gone for a witch, she will go boldly. If she is to be burned for a witch she will die singing. Her smoke will drift across the moon, mauve in the night storm. The winter winds would wail for her and the wild wood remember her wandering.

She laughed at them, at those high-minded and sober commissioners.

For sure she is a witch, she says, and the Devil is with her, she says. She is laughing.

How many of the men feel themselves hardening, rising to the teasing laughter that they have risen to before?

He creeps into our purses; he wriggles up our slits, when our monthlies no longer wash our wickedness away, she says. The Devil does, she says, rocking in her wild mirth.

How many of the men long to lower a hand to comfort their terrified pricks, which have been where the Devil has been?

Their terror and their shock make her laugh louder.

Can you cast a malfeasance? They ask. Of, course, she says.

Can you lay a sickness on a child? A love charm on a man? A blight on sheep and cattle? They ask. Easily, she says.

Do you welcome the Devil to your bed? They ask. All along with plenty of others, she says.

Can you . . . but they don't want to mention the fishing boat, that is too much, and she had been at home all the night, though singing and laughing of course . . . but that is too frightening, too big, it will cause too much stir. Too many questions will be asked, they will look little and silly in front of the Edinburgh men. They, the Commissioners, are gentlemen and scholars and cannot themselves believe such foolishness.

Can you . . . fly? They ask.

Oh yes, she says, we fly like straw whenever we please. Wild straw and corn straw are horses for us and we put them between our foot and say 'Horse and Hattock in the Devil's name'.

She can hardly subdue her laughter. She can hear the gasp of fear; she can see the tremor of terror, even on the faces of these cold and stupid men. This is a girls' game, and girls will be girls and the boys will be frightened.

Oh, yes, she says. When we want to ride, she says, we take windle-straws from bean stakes and say thrice:

'Horse and hattock, horse and gre,

Horse and pellake, ho ho.

And away in the Devil's name. Ho ho.'

Idiots, she thinks. It's as easy as that, she says. If you have the power.

So of course they killed her. They had to, but they would have done anyway. She is still laughing as the thin cord tightens. She had never learned properly how to be afraid and now it was too late to learn at all. Fifty years old and laughing in the wind.

Issobel Gowdie is gone for a witch

The laughter is disturbing. We had not believed it. Not really. Women must burn for witchcraft, but it is just an old game, a game from childhood that perhaps we are all too old to play. Boys will be boys and girls must put up with it.

We had not really believed it. But out of her own mouth and laughing . . .

How scared we must all have been: the men who fucked her, the women who scorned her.

And what of the Commissioners, with their new-fangled ways and civilised cynicism: William Dallas of Cantry, Sheriff Depute of Nairn; Master Harry Forbes, Minister of Auldearn; Alexander Brodie, younger, of Leathen; and all the other respectable Commissioners? What of them?

Did they look askance at their own wives when they went home to bed that night?

Did they give the next crazy beggar at their door a nervous smile and a cup of water, just in case?

But Issobel Gowdie is gone for a witch, flying free across the silver moon in the sharp air of a long May night.

☾ Issobel Gowdie is a historical figure – a woman of Auldearn, brought to trial for witchcraft by a Privy Council Commission in May 1662. We know very little more about her life. She was married, although, as women in Scotland at that time did not take their husbands' names, we do not know to whom she was married. We do not even know the outcome of her trial – although trials by commissioners had a very low acquittal rate.

We do know that under all the pressures, she found a way through of her own. Her spell for flying is recorded in the annals. It appears to have no parallels anywhere. I believe she made it up, for 'needs must where the Devil drives'.

What we know of her and her historical context can be studied in *Enemies of God* by Christina Larner (Blackwell, 1981), to whom much thanks.

Sailing the High Seas

~

MY MOTHER IS A PIRATE.

My mother is a pirate and for twenty years she has sailed down the salt seas of my dreams.

As for me now, I am not a pirate. I am a wife and a mother, and a storyteller. For money, and with pleasure, I tell stories: Black Jack and the mountain dwarves, lost maidens and fairy godmothers, the stone monkey in the hand of god, elves under the hill, Pan and his nymphs in the woods and the Romany folk a-tip-toe down the old roads. I do not tell stories of pirates though, not in the open, not out loud. Never.

But my mother is a pirate and she dips through the tropics by the palm green shores, swashing her buckle through coral shallows and Caribbean lagoons. Pearls in the hold, glowing in the hurricane's eye, emeralds, diamonds and gold moidores. At her masthead flutters the Jolly Roger, the skull and cross bones of her calling. She is laughing with Ann Bonney and Mary Reed. A green parrot is on her shoulder, as green as her green eyes; shivering timbers with a yo-ho-ho and a bottle of rum.

No. No, she stands, on the front of a dhow, legs straddled, arms akimbo, in camouflage combats with the sleeves rolled up to show the freckles and golden hair on her tanned arms. She has a Kalashnikov on a worn leather strap around her shoulder; she has heisted sophisticated weaponry from the Imperialist lackeys, the running dogs of capitalism, and now she delivers the precious cargo to the freedom fighters on the island.

No. No, her hair is grey and short now and she sits in an office in Marseilles in a chic little suit and silk scarf round her neck, and she shifts little pins on a map of the world that show the slow and crafty movement of heroin across the earth's oceans and along the veins of the damned. She speaks in perfect French to the Portuguese manager of the Italian-American Mafia she deals for. Then after work she goes to the Symphony on the arm of an elderly Austrian count.

No. No, in a small enclosed craft like an oyster shell, that hits each wave with a slap, she and her comrades, the eco-warriors, ram their way between the greedy, greasy whaler and the great singing innocents of the arctic ocean. The seal mothers watch gratefully from their ice floes, tuck their cream-white babies closer against their fishy breasts and comfortably recall the doom of the Titanic.

No. No, she rides a crimson water bike and with her irrepressibly laughing partner – a beautiful black gangster from New Orleans, with a gold tooth and a sharp crack – she boards smart yachts off Florida and teasing, joking, removes the diamonds from the flubbery necks of American fat cats, who do not know whether to laugh at such an adventure – a treasure more sparkly than jewels at the cocktail parties that Fall down the Keys – or whine at the loss of their toys.

No. No, she rides the long grey swell down the long grey coast, her arm round the dragon's neck and the red sail set square above her horned helmet. The holy hermits of the eastern isles beg for mercy, but she rampages, pillages, loots and burns. Freya, Goddess of War, rides on her shoulder, their pale faces lit by the smoking torches, and their hair blown back on the biting wind. The fierce look in her green eyes turns dreams to nightmares.

My mother is a pirate, but since my father smiled his last silent secret smile and died two years ago I know she does none of these things.

My mother is a pirate in the last place in the world you can still be a professional pirate – in Insulinde, the islands that drape the Equator like a necklace of jade. She lives by the quick, as they said of Moll Cutpurse, operating out of some small and hidden harbour in the Riau Archipelago, at the south-eastern end of the Malacca Straits, where a thousand tiny islands dot the busiest shipping lanes of the world. Here is the meeting and passing place of the trade routes into and out of Singapore, Sumatra, Java, Madura, Sulawesi; on a line between India and Australia; the way through from Vietnam and Hong Kong to the Indian Ocean. The islands of the Riau Archipelago, tossed up by casual volcanoes from the sea floor, have white sand beaches, living corals and dangerous reefs and shallows. The fisher villages walk down on stilts to the shore and paddle there, in the warm clear water. Hidden among those wooden pylons, lurking behind Chines junks, outdated cargo vessels, Bugi *prahu,* Sulawesian fishing craft and Sumatran *nade,* my mother has a high-powered motor launch, with a low-slung, streamlined cabin and a tripod-mounted machine gun on its white foredeck.

Her crew is a motley mixture of Bugi – the fierce seafaring people from the southern Celebes – and *orang laut,* the sea gypsies from nowhere at all except the sea, who are born and live and die on their scattered small craft and are buried at sea without ceremonies or gravemarkers. My mother rules these unruly people through her commanding height, through the wildness of her hair and the greenness of her eyes. And what they do is not very romantic, not truly, not at bottom: it is criminal and vicious and dangerous. They slip out under the purple clouds of sunset and lay alongside cumbersome cargo carriers, low-bellied ships laden to the gunnels, for the Plimsoll line is not much enforced in these waters. They clamber aboard, armed and threatening. Usually the fat drunken captains think only of the insurance money they have paid out over the years and readily hand over the hold keys or the smaller crates, and my mother's crew load them on to the motor launch and roar away into the darkness. But sometimes the captain is young and dreaming; or the vessel is his own; or he is more afraid of his Singapore boss than of any pirates on the high seas; or he has a swagger in his heart; or his pride cannot stand to be taken by a woman. He resists and orders his crew to resist and my mother and her gang shoot them all dead and scupper the ship. Sometimes for amusement or revenge or a need for speed, she has the captain and his whole crew thrown overboard to take their chances in the perilous waters. Then she runs, gun in hand, to the wheelhouse and revs up the engine of the unmanned craft and, leaping down into her own launch, sends it roaring off into the dark at high speed, crashing its way through the shipping lanes – as dangerous, uncontrolled and lethal as she is.

But, oh and the wideness of her smile, and the wildness of her hair and the length of her legs in her leather trousers, and the gold tan brown of her forearms, and the tiny dry lines like rays from the corners of her green, green eyes.

She is seventy-two now and my father is dead, so perhaps she has retired. Perhaps she has retired and plays on the white beaches with the golden youths who were once her crew. The grey streaks in her hair are indistinguishable from the white-gold ones that the sun has bleached out, and her collarbones stand out like spars above the neck of her T-shirt. Or she wears a silk tunic with a stand-up collar and loose baggy trousers, like a Chinese woman. She claps her hands and her boys run to serve her, and she eats spiced prawns marinated in ginger, and licks the garlic from her fingers and turns to the fat Chinese merchant who keeps her, and they laugh together in a language I do not know and inhale the sweet opium smoke that slits up her green, green eyes.

I know these things because when my father died my sister and I found a filing cabinet in the back of the garage. And in the filing cabinet were newspaper cuttings from *The Straits Times, The Sumatran Chronicle;* reports from obscure Lloyds syndicates, and the Malaysian police force; articles from *The Singapore Evening Herald* and *Indonesia Today.* They were all filed neatly and cross-referenced tidily. There was not one word about my mother, not even about a European pirate woman who terrorised the Straits of Malacca, but we knew my father did not collect all this for nothing. In the filing cabinet, also, was his passport with fully up-to-date visas for the more obscure corners of the East Indies; and a timetable of flights to the Far East; and well ordered stacks of bank notes in currencies we had never heard of. There were telephone numbers with notes for maritime or even criminal lawyers, and a small handbook on International Law and Piracy on the High Seas, which remains a capital offence even in Britain.

We knew he had not been abroad in twelve years, and then only to take one of his grandchildren for a weekend trip to look at the Renaissance. But he had been ready. For twenty years he had been ready to go if my mother needed him. In the meantime, he smiled his secret smile and was content.

We decided not to tell anyone about the filing cabinet, especially not my husband.

My mother is a pirate and for twenty years she has sailed down the salt seas of my dreams.

My mother has been a pirate for more than twenty years – avasting her way down the Malacca Straits and haunting my dreams with strange longings. But she was not always a pirate; not born to the craft and raised to the trade; not a pirate, woman and girl, and the daughter of pirates, living as such a woman must if the salt is in her blood and the sea wind rocked her cradle. No indeed. She was the daughter of an Anglican clergyman. The wife of a headmaster. The mother of two daughters. A primary schoolteacher. A good club tennis player beginning to turn her attention to golf. A soprano in the church choir. A loyal friend and a good neighbour. A woman who did not care for sewing, but was an excellent cook. I remember.

Now she is a pirate.

She was good at those things – I mean the things before. I was almost thirty when she left; these are not the memories of childhood that waver and re-form and are structured by fear and desire and given shapes and names because the little one needs stories that will fit. No, these are photographs – the clear and specific recall by a bright and educated woman of the day her mother became a pirate.

My parents met, they told us, walking on a beach in the West Highlands of Scotland. They appeared to each other from the opposite ends of a long pebble beach on Skye and walked towards each other in soft grey rain. By the time they reached the middle of the beach and each other, before they had even spoken, they both knew they were going to be married. They say. I doubt it myself. Be that as it may, and who can tell now, they were married, by her father, in his parish church, and for thirty-one years they were very happy.

I was born and when I was seven my sister was born. Sometimes my mother stayed at home with us and sometimes she was a primary schoolteacher. My father advanced in his career and eventually became a head teacher.

We lived such an ordinary, middle-class life, though happy. If your parents are happy, you do not ask yourself if they are happy; you hardly ask yourself if you are happy. But now I know that they were happy and I was happy. My father was head-teacher of a Special School near Peterborough. A Special School is one for pupils who cannot, for whatever reason, be accommodated within the normal educational curriculum: his were young people with emotional and behavioural problems of a moderate kind. Borderline. He was, I understand, good at it. We lived in an old village just over the county boundary into Northamptonshire. So it cannot have been the everlasting wind that sweeps over the Fens, bringing icy air direct from the Ural Mountains to the centre of Peterborough, that got into my mother's bones and turned her wild. I went to school and was in the Brownies though not the Girl Guides and I rode a pony for a while and then I didn't any more, but my sister took it over so we did not have our girlish hearts broken. Etcetera. Etcetera. It isn't meant to sound boring, but ordinary.

The only thing that was not ordinary about my parents was that often when my father looked at my mother he would smile, a gentle smile full of an amusement so deep that you knew it would be impossible to get the joke unless you were my father. He was the gentlest man I have ever known, but he had this secret joke that no one shared. Maybe she did, my mother, or maybe she was the joke, but either way it was a good joke, not cruel or mean, but belly-deep and joyful. Except that when you are growing up you don't notice the silly faces your father makes, especially if he is a head teacher, than which there is no greater shame, not if you are a teenager and it is the nineteen-sixties.

So I grew up and I left home and went out into the world to seek my fortune. Later I met an amazing man and the most amazing thing about him was that he wanted to marry me.

'Don't,' said my parents when I told them.

'Why not?' I asked.

'He doesn't smile when he looks at you,' said my father gently.

'That's why,' I said crossly.

'He won't let you go,' said my mother.

'That's why,' I said crossly.

I married him and they smiled at each other and were very nice about my not doing what I was told.

So then I was not living at home; but my sister still was for a while, working her way through A-levels and being a teenager and then she went off to Oxford. (I have forgotten to mention that she was extremely brainy, my little sister, but actually this has very little to do with this story.) But we have, not surprisingly, talked and talked about it and both of us are certain that their marriage did not collapse with the departure of their daughters. On the contrary, there was a deep and delicate delight in them both, which seemed to deepen in their solitude.

A few weeks before my mother's fiftieth birthday, my father rang and said would I come to visit that particular weekend. I had planned to go anyway, because it was her birthday and because I had some news of my own that I wanted to tell them. Then my father said,

'Could you come without James?' and after a pause he added, 'Please.'

I thought they were being sentimental old idiots really, but as it happened James was going to be away that weekend anyway, so I did not make a fuss. I drove up on the Sunday morning, the very birth date itself, and because it was convenient I picked my sister up at Peterborough station *en route.* We hugged and giggled as always. We get on very well and we always have.

'You're looking unusually pleased with yourself,' she said as I drove the car over the A1 and on to the Oundle road.

'Yes,' I said almost smirking.

'Me too,' she said. I looked at her and she did look rather smug. 'News?'

'Do you mind if I keep it? Sort of so it can be a birthday present for Mummy.'

'Good idea,' I said, 'mine too.'

So we drove in peaceful accord to my parents' house. It was a sunny summer's day and when we arrived my father was mowing the lawn and my mother was arranging a picnic lunch on the patio and it all looked so secure and sweet. They were so sweet, my parents. Then there was much hugging and congratulating and kissing and present-giving and popping of corks from mediocre champagne bottles and chattering and then my sister took a deep breath and said,

'I heard yesterday. I got my First and they've confirmed the Yale scholarship.' You could see them both glow with pride. It was a wonderful present for my mother; it did truly make them both even happier.

I said, 'And I'm pregnant.' And that was a wonderful birthday present too. Her green eyes filled with tears of delight, and my father looked at her and smiled his secret smile and gave a tiny nod. She stood up, and suddenly I remembered, or re-realised, how tall she was.

She paused for a moment, her hands on the back of my father's chair. For that moment, for a tiny second in the sunshine I think she was nervous. I think she wavered, almost wavered, or perhaps she was nervous only about the telling and never about the doing. I don't know. Then she drew a deep breath, placed a little kiss on my father's head, straightened up and said, 'That's perfect. It's perfect. It ties almost everything up. Now I can be off to be a pirate.' She turned from the table and walked into the house.

'What?' said my sister into the stunned moment.

I thought, I really did think, she had said 'pilot'. I thought my father had given her flying lessons for her birthday present. I thought that was a fabulous present. I thought perhaps James would give me flying lessons and she and I could play aerial acrobatics together. Though not until after the baby was born, of course. I turned to my father to congratulate him, and was silenced.

I have never . . . no one ever . . . there is no word for that expression . . . for my father's face then and its loss and love and pride and loneliness and through all that and within it and inseparable from it, a profound hilarity; the laughter of mountains and storms, a complete and hard-earned joy. I felt as though I had walked into their bedroom and found them having sex. I was intruding into an intimacy I had not even dreamed of. I knew only with a kind of sudden bitterness that James would never, ever feel anything remotely like that for me.

'What?' said my sister again, 'Did she say 'pirate'?'

I was still dumbfounded. But my father nodded and said, 'Yes. Yes she did.' He reached over the table and took my sister's hand. 'Be generous,' he said, 'try to be generous. She's put it off for a long time because she loves us.' Then he laughed, laughed aloud with pure delight and when my sister looked quizzically at him, he spluttered out that he could not wait to hear what the vicar would say.

There was a ferocious roar from behind the house and my mother, in red biker leathers, swept round the garden on a huge snarling brand-new black motorbike, kicking up the raked gravel in front of the house. My father stood and held up a detaining hand; he was grinning broadly. He walked over to my mother where she straddled the bike, its engine still running.

'This,' he said, looking at the manic machine, 'is showing off.'

'Yes, I know,' she said, 'but I could hardly call for a taxi.'

'No. Well it's a classy exit. Have you got a licence?'

'I'm a pirate,' she shouted, 'I don't need a licence.'

'Well, put your helmet on,' he said.

They hugged, briefly, closely, and then she put on the helmet, which was hanging from the handlebars. He did up the strap under her chin, exactly as he had done up our straps when we went pony riding as children, tapping her on the head when the job was done. He stepped back. She growled the engine loudly, grinned at the two of us still on our patio chairs, and accelerated out through the white painted gates to be a pirate.

I have never seen her again.

'She ran off,' they said. 'Poor man,' they said. My father smiled his secret smile.

'She died,' they murmured. 'He can't even bear to talk about it, the poor man.' He smiled, shrugging his shoulder.

'She's a lesbian,' they whispered. 'She went off with that gym teacher. I ask you. Poor man.' He grinned.

'He killed her,' they muttered. 'He bashed her head in and buried her under the patio.' My father's smile deepened, pulling the fine lines round his eyes into arrowheads.

'Daddy,' I tried once, only once, 'Daddy, aren't you ever angry with her?'

'Angry?' He sounded quite genuinely surprised. 'Why ever would I be angry? She gave me thirty-two years – not bad, eh? No, not angry . . . grateful sometimes, but I suppress it, she wouldn't like that.' He smiled, deep and private and joyful. 'No, she never 'wasted my precious time'."

My father never seemed to need to discuss it. As though he had always known that one day she would go off to be a pirate. He never saw her again either. But about five years later she sent him a birthday present: a pair of gold cufflinks, heavy, solid. Each had two circles touching each other.

'An "S"?' I asked. 'Tear drops?'

'No,' he said, 'don't be silly. They're eights. Pieces of eight.' And he laughed. He never took them off. Sometimes he would fiddle with them, touching and turning them as he sat watching the cricket on the television, or walking in his garden or reading. He would smile his secret smile and you knew that he was still happy

I have gone over and over it with my sister of course. We have wondered and speculated and been sad and curious and have missed her and hated her and loved her and envied her. We have been angry on our own behalf, on her grandchildren's behalf, and on grounds of abstract morality, but we cannot be angry on his behalf. Sometimes, and I must confess my sister is better at this than I am, sometimes we are even amused, catch that deep hilarity and joy that my father found in my mother. I catch my sister smiling a secret smile and know she is on to something that I haven't quite grasped yet.

It is my fiftieth birthday next month. This brings strange longings and losses to a woman. I find I have bizarre regrets: why didn't I have eight children? Become a contemplative nun? Make lots of money? Live in Istanbul? And even more bizarre ambitions: I want to breed poisonous fungi, have lots of sex, become a pilot, buy an aquarium, get a tattoo, be an arctic explorer and become a grandmother.

I want to have a lover who will look at me with deep and abiding mirth and will let me go with hilarity and delight, a man who loves the pirate soul in me. As things stand I worry that when I stop bleeding I will not be able to tell stories any more. I worry that I will stop dreaming too and will never again be able to pursue my mother down the salt seas of my dreams.

Foreplay

MY LOVER HAS SILVER WINGS above his ears. I find them enchanting, but he does not like to have them mentioned.

My lover has a ribbon, a twisted purple ribbon that runs across the white skin of his belly, across the contours of his white chest, just below the small hard cranberry of his right nipple and up into the silky hair of his armpit. A savage wound that must have hurt twice, once in the getting and once in the healing. He already had this long puckered scar when I first saw him, but I did not see it for nearly half a century.

My lover and I have found a way to send each other messages, in perfect security – safe even from betrayal by each other, or theft, or threat or blackmail. I have a small box, wrought silver on ebony, like my lover's hair. My husband gave it to me long ago, when my golden hair still shone soft in the candle light and bright in the sunshine. My husband gave me a box, and I use it to send secret messages to my lover. It has two intricate fastenings, each different, gates and wards of my secret places. When I wish to send my lover a message I place it in the box my husband gave me; and I lock one of the fastenings with a key that never leaves me, and I seal it with my seal. Then I send it to my lover at the hand of a page; and when the page finds my lover, which can often take some time, he gives him the box. My lover takes his key, which is different from mine, which never leaves him and which I have never seen, and locks and seals the second fastening. Then he sends it back to me. I break my seal, unlock the lock that my key fits and send the box to him once more. And when he receives it, he can use his key to unlock the fastening that he himself locked, and so, at last find out my message. The keys we guard with our lives. I do not know where he keeps his, but, wrapped in a piece of oiled leather, I keep mine inside my body, so that my lover is always with me there, always inside me; there is no end to his physical presence for me, and this pleases me. I only take it out when my husband comes to me at night, and this happens seldom now. Oh, and of course, when my lover and I find the quiet moment, the shadowed place, the unwatched and unguarded hour; and then I have no need of a key. This does not happen often either.

Often we laugh together, my lover and I, for despite all this care and attention, there is rarely anything we need to send each other. Sometimes I put jokes in the box and send my lover's page out on all this lengthy rigmarole to deliver nothing but an apple with one bite taken out; or a piece of parchment with a snail trail, a thumb-smear of my body's juices, for I am juicy even though I am not fruitful.

Sometimes he sends me a white rose, faded and withered by the time I finally get to open the box, a black pubic hair, bold and springing. Like all the knights of Camelot there remains something boyish, something nursery-playful about my lover. And therefore also about our games of love, even in our sin, even in the harsh wastelands where I go and am pierced by him deep inside, and ravaged by the cold steel that he and I heat red and white in the forge of our desire.

There is more than a joke to it though. The passagings of our box fill time, take time, bring everything down to slowness, extend the waiting, nourish the wanting, and this is how it is and has always been for us. Our desire has been fed on delay, retreat, denial, on cold waiting not hot acting. My lover and I have enjoyed the longest foreplay of any lovers in history. Thirty-four years, four months and eleven days between when our eyes first met and the consummation of the desire that was born there, then, there at that moment, there in that glance, in that silent, humble, unexpected, unwanted glance for which in the end I believe the whole realm of Logres, all the brave bright hope of Camelot, all the care and love and work and thought of my husband, will go up in smoke and be lost forever.

I do not care.

Now I care only for that glance, that meeting melting moment; and if knights must die for it, then, frankly, that is what knights are for. And if kingdoms are lost for it, then say I, I will stand on the battlements of a ruined castle as I stood then, and shout out that this is a better way to go than in the silly squabbles of an heirless palace when an old king turns his face to wall and dies.

I was a child when he came, a child with a long fat tail of plaited hair that slapped against my back when I skipped rope in the courtyard of my father's castle and envied my brothers when they came in from hunting. I was a child when he came and taught still by the raucous laughter, the healthy contempt and the chattering gossip of nurses and servants. I was a child not yet promoted to the shining stillness of my mother's chamber where she sat among her maidens and her white hands moved gentle over spindle or harp string.

I was no longer a child when he came, although my long fat tail of plaited hair still slapped against my back when I skipped rope in the courtyard of my father's castle. Three months before that glittering cavalcade rode up the long defile from the flood plain, a young squire – for this was too great a matter for pages or hired hands – had galloped down to the river and I had stood on the wall and watched him go. Under his leather jerkin he carried a small package and in the package was a cloth stained red-brown with my first menstrual blood, a gift to Arthur, King of Britain, from my Father, the Lord Guardian of the Northern Passes, a gift promised since before I was conceived.

Child then and not-child, the news of the coming was brought to me by my father's page and I ran up the long staircase to my mother's chamber and there my mother waited on me. With her own hands she took off of the linen kirtle I wore and dressed me in green silk, and circled my waist with the great treasure of our house, the silver girdle which they say the Magdalen herself had laid aside when she ceased whoring and followed Our Good Lord to Calvary. My mother unplaited my long hair, and it rippled in unaccustomed freedom. I could see the pride in her eyes, which I had never before seen for me, but only for my brothers.

She laughed a little and made me a small courtesy and said, not wholly mocking, 'Well, little Queen, if you don't tell your father, you may run up the gateward-tower and watch him coming.'

So I stood on the parapet in the late afternoon sun and I watched him ride towards me; so fine and lovely, black hair and white face and silver armour. There was then, then and still, something wild and shadowed about him, a kind of feverish intensity. He and his party rode into the outer bailey and the horses clattered on the cobbles and he looked up suddenly and our eyes met. One glance. One glance between a romantic young woman and a romantic young man and more young women will weep for it and more young men will die for it than for any glance there has ever been.

And I do not repent. I rejoice.

They did not tell me, no one bothered to tell me, that Arthur, that the High King of All Britain, would not ride up a rocky defile in the northern mountains to fetch away his child bride himself. My glance was open, my smile unveiled because I believed it was my husband that I smiled at. And later, when the choirs sang and the bells and trumpets sounded and I walked in solemn procession up the great cathedral nave and was welcomed by a huge golden stranger who smiled, it was too late. He should not have sent Lancelot to fetch me; he should have sent someone else. He could have sent someone else; and any man not wrapped in the power of his own kingship would have sent someone else, to bring a child from the nursery and the bride to his bed.

For three weeks we rode southwards, with my father's kisses still warm on my cheeks, and his final blessing – *'Go forth and be the mother of many princes, to the glory of God and Britain'* – still sweet in my ears. We rode southwards through the springing of the year. Each day I rode behind Lancelot, my hair brushing the white skin of his neck, my cheek pressed against the valley between his hard shoulders, my arms around his waist. We rode then as we sleep now on the rare occasions that we can. The days were lengthening and sunny; primroses and the white wind flowers bloomed under trees that were pink-budded and fat with promise of a new summer; and daisies and cowslips danced on the meadows beneath the horses' feet, and birds sang all around us. How could it have been otherwise? Why did Arthur send Lancelot, when he could have sent so many others and we could have ridden southwards forever and stirred nothing but the roadway dust in our passing?

Right from the start we learned the artful delight of waiting; of delay, of silence, pretence, evasion. Of guile. Each evening he would lift me slowly against his body. As my toes touched the ground I would pause one tiny moment longer that necessary before letting them take my weight and he and I would be pressed against each other, doing standing up what is better done lying down. That was all.

Let me be clear. Let me be very clear, here at least. It was not love. Not then and never since. It was desire, and why not? It was not sin. Someone else, not he nor I, someone else, God if you must, made two bodies, my body and his body, made them with the precise turnings of jaw bones and cheeks, the exact timbres of voices, the very shapes of penis and vagina that meant we could not and cannot look at each other without our stomachs churning, dampness flooding out of me – so that some evenings I am embarrassed to rise from my chair leaving a dark stain on the seat – and hardness rising in him.

It was not love. It might be easier if it were love. Love has an imperative, love has and confers right. But no, it was lust; a simple little thing that feels enormous and ought to be unimportant. I did not love him, although in that childish springtime I did not know there was a difference and I would have called it love if I had ever tried to find words. I never loved him. If I did any loving, and I have never done much, it was and is and always will be Arthur I loved. Love is strange, a beautiful and complicated thing that leads to self-denial and care and tenderness. It breeds laughter and deep friendship. It does not, not of itself, lead towards the thrashing legs, the moans and grunts and giggles, the murmuring, turning, lapping of tongues, the imperious demands. Love does not make those panting, thrusting, rising sounds, that sigh, that high triumphant cry of satisfactory sexual coupling.

I loved Arthur, as I love him still – my king, my husband, my friend. I loved him in a seemly, mannerly way. A warm, thoughtful, civil, civilised love. And so I love him still. But in all those years of loving the itch, the longing to scratch, the flea on my skin, inside my underclothes never went away. Poor Lancelot, more self-deluding than I am, might try still to call it love, he would like to have that excuse; but, sadly for him, he is not as stupid as sexually beautiful men so often are. Once in our secret box I sent him a flea. A tease, a joke and he paid me in kind. He sent me back a well-blooded strip of cloth, a woman's monthly cloth, and he marked it clearly with a red cross – his sign, his emblem by which he may be known even in battle.

I loved Arthur, but I could not love him enough to quench the thirst of the greedy mouth between my legs. Because, from the start, I loved him as something he would never be.

I loved him as the father of my child.

They say all barren women are bitter. The soured *vinaigre* of their empty wombs purses up their lips, and makes them sharp and mean. This is a lie. There is no knight in Camelot, no serving wench within the walls, who has ever seen a shadow on the Queen's smile; who has ever seen in her anything but a serene and gracious presence. She is not sharp, but soft and the trailing of her hem along the rushed floor of the Great Hall is musical.

I wanted that child. I watched women with their children. I saw the velvet-down round heads of the new-born babies, as round as the spinning globe. I heard the soft bubbling noises of the nursing infants and the high-pitched, demanding chatter of the weans. I saw the boys, still milk-soft at eight or nine, patting a mother's cheek as they ran past her through the Hall, or leaning against her as she sat at table, making swift tender gestures that they hoped their friends would not notice. I saw the girls, giggling together, gaggled, admiring each other and themselves and their developing high courage and nobility. I saw the parents' pride as their children came to adulthood and took their places in the hunt, the battle, the quest and were given their seats at the Round Table. Dear God, I saw the same pride on Lancelot's own face when Galahad came to court. Galahad who ought to have been his father's shame, young and lovely, walking up the hall with just that lordly stride that Lancelot has, and despite him being golden like the Fair Elayne, there was no one in that vast chamber who did not know exactly what had passed between that Lady and Sir Lancelot du Lac. Lancelot's every feature in pink and gold instead of black and silver was printed on the youth and it was delightful to see. His father's glow was delightful too. Even now, sometimes, even when he is looking at me, when his desire is hot on him, his gaze will flicker, a half-smug half-humble smile will curl his lips, and without looking over my shoulder, I will know that Galahad has come in to the room.

I wanted that.

And . . . and something else, something more . . . it was for that child that Lancelot had been sent a three-week journey into the north to fetch me. *'Go forth and be the mother of many princes,'* my father bade me as he blessed me, *'to the glory of God and Britain.'* A high calling, and if it was not my calling, then why did I not stay happy and clam in the northlands? Marry some Lord of the Marches and live a useful life? Or, if he were killed in some border skirmish, go to some convent and live in peace?

Both my sisters have done those things and are well and happy in the doing of them, but for me the choirs in the cathedral sang and the bells and trumpets sounded, and my hand – tiny and soft in their large hard hands – was given by my lover, who had fetched me from my father, to my husband who received me in the presence of five bishops and all the court of Camelot. This did not happen for some fourteen-year-old with a long pigtail, however gold-shining. No, this all happened for the Queen, the mother of the future King, the mother of God's prince and valiant champion, the Mother of Britain.

There was no child.

No one had thought of this. It had not occurred to any of them when they made their plans way back before my conception. It had not occurred to me as a matter of fact.

At first no one worried.

Later 'she is young,' they said, 'it is not good for women to be brought to bed before they have finished growing. She is young.'

Later there were disturbances on the eastern coast, the Norsemen's dragon-ships harrying the fisher folk. 'The King has been away the better part of the year,' they said, 'but when he comes home . . .'

Later 'My Lady,' they said, 'does the King . . . ?' their voices trailed away embarrassed, for it is both funny and frightening to think that when the king goes to his wife's bedroom and strips off his hose, his bottom is as hairy and his limp penis as ludicrous as any other man's. When the King – our noble and victorious ruler – and the Queen – our pure and lovely child-bride – go to the work of making baby princes there is the same sweating and farting, the same panting and heaving, the same wet patch on the under-sheet as any other couple. The King's come is as cheesy in the grey dawn, the Queen's slit as sticky, as any groom's or chambermaid's.

'Does the King . . . ?' they ask. 'Yes, he does,' I say quickly, fiercely. And he does. We both do. We work hard on it for years, both of us, the desire for the prince overriding any shortage of desire for each other.

Each month, with perfect discretion so that neither the King nor I will have to speak about it, the chief lady of my chamber took the first drops of my period blood on a white handkerchief and gave them to the King's page who silently offered them to his liege lord, and the *Te Deums* and holidays that wait only on a pure white unspotted cloth are postponed again, for one more month.

There was no child.

There was no child.

Gradually, as Arthur's chest slipped downwards towards his waist and his bulk both expanded and softened; gradually as the network of little lines spread and deepened round my nose and eyes, as the soft skin of my upper arms turned flabby; gradually, as a whole new generation of young men grew from children to pages, from pages to squires, were knighted and in their turn took their seats at the Round Table; so gradually that there was no way to note the moment, the court gave up hope and practised resignation instead.

Arthur and I rarely spoke about it. We went on trying, though fitfully. Once after nearly twenty years he said, 'Guinevere, you . . . you must not think I love you less because you never had my children.' So then I knew that he did love me less or he would not have thought of it. I loved him less; there was less of him to love. I could love the king, the husband, the friend, but I could not love the father, as had been planned.

He turned away from me slowly. He became a father to the young men – a good father, I think; and I mourned for the son who did not have him as a father. You could see him surrounded by all that physical youth and adoration and he handled it wisely. Camelot was lovely in those years. But I could not be a mother to the young men because they wanted the virgin queen, their pure and distant icon, not a cuddly old woman. It is boring to be a pure icon the whole time; to accept the trophies laid at one's feet and smile sweetly on each and every one of them equally until they find a wife for themselves and give up boyish devotions. And because of them I could not be a mother to the young women either – no young woman chooses a mother whom all the young men are in love with, however chastely. It is boring to be treated with a mixture of awe and suspicion; to lull the fears and act with perfect decorum while being beautifully dressed, until they find a husband for themselves and assume a look of superiority and compassion.

So I was a busy queen and a bored woman. All this time I desired Lancelot. He desired me. We never spoke of it. We were both waiting. It was there, always. We played elaborate games that nourished the fire. Slow games with unwritten rules: we would not catch each other's eye at a meal. We must look at the other, but the one who is looking must not be seen to be looking by the one who is looked at. Such games. They are fun in a dark and shadowed way. They feed the flames. We never spoke of it.

Lancelot, the King's Right Hand, and, of course, the Queen's Champion, who wore her favour in his helmet although such courtly gestures were no longer in fashion, was the perfect knight. This was the habit, the ritual, the liturgy of the court. This, like the Queen's beauty and her devotion to the King, underpinned the power, the prestige of Camelot, were an integral part of the great bulwark that Arthur of Britain had built against the Eastern peril. Even Lancelot himself was fooled by it. So we were held within the limits of our own game, the unacknowledged, silent game that we played for more than thirty years.

And then they all went out on the Quest of the Holy Grail. A great foolishness, it was. We had the threat of the Norsemen so pinned down on the eastern coasts that there was not much to do. The captains of the dragon-ships were offering to trade instead of ravage; to turn us into merchants instead of warriors. The noble Knights of the Round Table had not learned to accommodate the days of boredom; so they upped the stakes, and gambled on holiness, for which they had little training.

And while they were away something changed for me. A month passed, and then two, and I did not bleed. At first there was a flicker, a little flame of hope. I read the tales of Sarah, of Hannah and Elizabeth and I let hope spark up in my heart. I was forty-seven years old and the faces of my women told me differently.

I was a barren woman, queen of a barren womb, and the days of hope and prayer were all passed. I would go down into the long shadows of old age with nothing better to show for my years than a sweet and patient resignation. Arthur would die and his rule would pass and Mordred would strut in his inheritance and I would be stuck by the fire, dribbling the inanities of senility and muttering a nostalgia for a golden age that had never existed.

I had been the perfect wife for nothing, for nothing.

I had been the sweet child and the lovely woman and the pure queen and all for nothing.

I had an enormous rage in me against the whole business of my life.

And something else changed. I do not know, I do not ask, what happened to Lancelot on the Quest of the Holy Grail, but he came home to Camelot defeated. He could no longer believe in himself as the perfect knight, and when he looked at Galahad there was a new bitterness tucked close and seamless alongside his pride. We talked one long evening of this and that, there seemed no new substance to the talk that there had not always been between him and me. But although we did not talk about it, we both knew that the other knew that self-denial, self-discipline, self-control had brought us nothing but their own dryness.

The next morning was bright. The sun rose innocent and sparkling. The King went hunting.

'Tell Sir Lancelot,' I ordered my page, before I even knew I was going to do it, 'Tell Sir Lancelot that his Queen wishes him to meet her in the cherry orchard.'

The cherry orchard wall is high. The cherry orchard grass is bright and green, spangled with flowers. I waited more impatiently than at any time since I had stood on the gateward tower of my childhood home and watched a knight on a black charger ride up at the head of a jingle-jangling cavalcade.

He came, smiling. The silver wings of hair above his ears made his black hair and white skin magical. He knelt, as he always does, even in private; playing his knightly role, he knelt graceful at my feet and raised the hem of my dress to his lips.

'How may this most humble of knights serve the most gracious of ladies?' There was a chuckle, almost a greedy giggle, in his voice, and I knew he knew and had consented.

I wanted to be the one. I wanted to make the move, take the decision, be the seducer. With great generosity, he let me.

Very slowly I reached out my hand, rested it on his dark head. I waited. He waited. We were used to waiting. Slowly I pushed my hand back through his hair; his head was heavy with the waiting. I could feel the top of his skull fitting into my palm as though it belonged there. For a long while it was so hard to move forward; to change the rules of our long game. There was a moment of stillness. Could we have stopped there? I do not know. A cock chaffinch sung his imperious mating call from a high branch.

I was wearing a gown that opened down the front; and I wore nothing underneath it that morning. 'Serve me like this,' I said, and reached out the other hand to encircle the back of his dark and shapely head. With both hands almost roughly I pulled his head towards my lower body, so that, half unbalanced, he stumbled nose first against my pubic bone and my dress fell open and his mouth encountered all the rich juice that had accumulated over thirty-four years, four months and eleven days of desire. On the green grass, he ate me, drank me, washed me clean, and I bridled him with my legs in unbridled passion. This was new, this was something I had never done before, never felt before. This was not how you made babies or friendship. This, as I was to learn quickly enough, was how you made orgasms.

I heard a cold, distant cry and for a moment did not recognise that it was my own voice crying out. I did not know that sound; it was not pain or joy. I cried out again, and recognised the sound of victory.

'Fuck me now,' I told him; and his surprise at hearing the word from his Gracious Queen brought him to orgasm so quickly that for the first time in his life he was unable to obey her command.

Experience has taught me that I like to suck even more than I like to be sucked. I like penetration – and of every orifice. I like to tease, to play games, to invent scenarios, to spank and to be spanked. I love to mutter to him in language so filthy that outside the hold of his arms I do not even know those words. I like everything that a pure and chaste queen is not supposed to like. I like it because I am not supposed to like it. I like it because I am old enough and wise enough to know that this is not love, it is simply lust and I like the feeling of the deep rocking inside, the high spiralling moment and the exhausted sweaty heap that the two of us become when the pulsing is over.

I send him delay in a secret box; our pages run about the countryside slowing things down to this slow moment. There is no hurry. He teases me, tantalises, holding back when I urge him, command him forward, controlling my moment, refusing to hurry; not yet . . . not yet . . . not yet . . . now. Ah, yes, the long sweet now.

We know that delay stokes up the fire of desire, we know that secrecy, evasion, suddenness, panic, even fears and the pains that our middle-aged bodies cannot escape, all pile up, slow how slowly towards a carnal satisfaction that is more than worth the waiting. So thus we send each other secret messages in a box, wrought silver on ebony, with two locks to which we each have one key.

I was faithful, so faithful, so long as there was any chance of being the mother of Arthur's child. But what can virtue offer me now that could measure up to the cherry orchard, to that cold triumphant cry and the soft quivering of happy flesh.

My lover has silver wings above his ears; he has beautiful veins of silver in the black mine of pubic hair that surrounds his beautiful prick. I find them enchanting, but I never tell him so. He does not like these signs of ageing, but I love them. They have set me free.

And if the whole realm of Logres burn for it; if Camelot is swallowed up in the waves of my passion; if we all go down into the dark and are forgotten; if my name becomes a byword for lascivious betrayal, I do not care.

I exult.

Empty Nest Syndrome

~

SHE WOKE UP TOO EARLY, restless and hungover; dry mouth, blurry eyes, a little nauseous, slightly achy. And tired: tired from the whole of the day before and tired again from sleeping badly. She had fallen semi-stuporous into her bed, but before sleep had reposed her she had been awake again. Her skin had itched as though all the insects in the universe were scuttling over it *en route* for some vile international hexapedal conference of their own, and she had sweated and sweated despite being dehydrated. So now she was restless and tired and hung over.

She crept out of bed, not wanting to stir the sleeping bulk beside her. She was, she thought, too old for all this, for Christmas cavorting, for any overlong evenings and especially for those passed in single malt tastings. She groped her way to the window and, pulling the curtain aside, looked out into a December dawn. Below her the garden glinted frost while the moon set in the west and a frail fringe of pink rimmed the eastern skyline. Between them was a purity of indigo, just barely beginning to pale.

It was magically silent. Behind her her husband slept. A solid shape beneath the duvet. Upstairs her daughter slept too, sprawled out in some extravagant arrangements of thin white limbs or, perhaps, tightly furled into the shoulder of her lover. At least she hoped her daughter slept. Last night her daughter had lost her virginity. The woman knew this as a fact, though without physical evidence. Indeed the knowing of it partially explained the hangover since much of the drinking had been a collusive effort by the woman, the daughter and the about-to-be lover to keep any clue to this impending event from the woman's husband, the daughter's father, the lover's host. None of them had wanted a drama and Christmas is, after all, for the children.

She leaned her weary aching head against the window-pane. She could just pick out the soft glow of the Christmas roses, the white hellebores creamily and considerately flowering on time. Further away the beloved and laboured-over garden was reduced to its basic forms; patches of dark, darker and darkest shapes moulded the night's own darkness. On the lawn beneath the window she saw that the Good Mother and the Bad Mother were engaged in a conversation.

The Bad Mother looks like Cruella de Vil, tall and aquiline, glamorous in a full-length flowing coat made not of dalmatian but of ocelot fur: the sexiest coat in all the world and the wickedest. Even in the half-dark the woman can see that the Bad Mother's fingernails are varnished vermilion and filed into long points. There are tiny grosgrain bows on the back of the Bad Mother's stiletto-heeled shoes; and from them the seams of silk stockings run straight upwards, disappearing under the soft fur and leading to a destination of french knickers and softer delights.

The Good Mother, by contrast, looks like the Pantomime fairy; dishevelled and plump and shabbily, deliberately, cuddly. The Good Mother holds the front edges of her spotless but shabby cardigan together with fingers that are adorned only by a single plain gold ring. Were it not dark her hands would appear scrubbed, clean or raw depending on perspective. For reasons not entirely clear she is wearing Wellington boots and has, so early in the morning is it, not yet had the opportunity to brush her hair. It fluffs around her face, the last scraps of an old perm not enough to give it shape. Though patently warm and sweet-natured, the Good Mother is slightly frazzled and absent-minded from the effort of constant self-sacrifice.

The two of them are having a post-Christmas-day grumble, at the world and at each other.

The Good Mother moans gently and says, 'You might have thought that after all my effort They could at least have offered to help with the washing up. They're so selfish.'

The Bad Mother snorts ferociously and says, 'You might have thought that They were old enough to know that the last thing I would want for Christmas is kitchen appliances. They're so selfish.'

They are agreed on something. This disconcerts them.

The Good Mother pats her plump but shapeless bosom and says, 'Of course I only do it for Them. Christmas is for children, I always say.' It is not immediately clear then why she sounds so whiny.

The Bad Mother fingers one ruby earring and says, 'Of course when They were younger They were rather sweet; it's adolescence that is so intolerable.' It is not immediately clear then why she sounds so triumphant.

They do manage to agree though that He is a selfish bastard, though not about why. The Good Mother thinks he is a selfish bastard because he doesn't give Them enough time or attention. The Bad Mother thinks he is a selfish bastard because he always sides with Them and gets Them over-excited. One way and another both He and They are the opposition, the enemy. The Good Mother and the Bad Mother are both isolated and fragile in the cold light of the morning; the frost and their tiredness making them sharp, with themselves and with each other.

They are both lonely. They turn, without trust but in need, to the other, their heads close together. The Bad Mother bends her slender neck downwards and the Good Mother thrusts both her chins upwards. They mutter low, telling women's secrets to each other.

The Good Mother mutters peevishly that she wrapped her own sexuality up in pretty paper, with silver ribbons and hand-crafted bows and tags. 'And I gave it to the Daughter, and, would you believe it, she just returned it saying quite politely, "Thank you, but I've got one of my own."' The Good Mother's voice is quivering on the edge of tears at such ingratitude.

The Bad Mother snarls aggressively that she sharpened her manicured talons and excised the Daughter's sexuality in a fine slashing movement, and hid it in her own brassiere. 'And the daughter stood there, and, do you know, she just laughed, saying quite calmly, "Plenty more where that one came from."' The Bad Mother's voice is grating on the edge of fury at such temerity.

The Daughter is invisible, but her presence causes the frost to snap at the two of them, as they stand in the garden and the rosy line of dawn widens and the brightness of the moon fades against a sky which has flowed unnoticed from indigo to eggshell blue. Crossly they turn away, not fleeing but departing. The scorn of the Daughter seems to have unknit them both. There is alarm now in their postures, for they have been overheard, spied on, caught out. Neither He nor They is the real enemy. The other is the other's enemy. And they have, both, been collaborating with the enemy.

The Good Mother stomps sullenly up the garden path; beside her the Bad Mother paces irritably. The garden path takes them across the silver lawn to the gate into the orchard. Here they pause, look guiltily around, then embrace, entwine and vanish.

The Good Mother suffers from unshiftable depression.

The Bad Mother suffers from uncontrollable rages.

'Tough,' exclaims the Woman. Her headache has been soothed by the cool glass of the windowpane. Suddenly she laughs, contemptuous of them both. 'And be damned to the pair of you,' she says. She leaves the window, climbs back into bed, puts her chilly arms around her husband, not caring that this makes him shiver and grunt softly. She kisses his shoulder and falls asleep, not even hearing the fine notes of the first blackbird in the morning.

Of Deborah and Jael

~

AFTERWARDS, WHEN THE WAR was over and the army disbanded, Deborah the Prophetess, a judge in Israel, returned to her place of judgement under the palm tree on the dusty road between Ramah and Bethel, under Mount Ephraim. She sat twice weekly with her feet tucked under her heavy thighs, her back as straight as a warrior's, and her hands half open, forming bowls of knowledge on her knees. And there the people of Israel, the northern tribes, came up to her for judgement: the men a little more nervously perhaps, and the women with sly smiles which she usually ignored. And sometimes, between the lambing and the travelling seasons, Jael would come down to visit Deborah, and would place her index fingers in the bowls of Deborah's hands. And Deborah would know, even as she prayed with her eyes shut, just from the feel of that pressure, that it was Jael who had come and they would laugh together like the young women.

Afterwards, when the war was over and the army disbanded, Deborah the Prophetess made a song for Jael the Kenite. A song of blood and blessing. Deborah made the song because it is the duty of the prophets to sing the triumphs and instil the stories by rhythm and repetition deep in the minds of the people, so that they need not be afraid. And she made the song for Jael because they were friends, and because they had both come a long way to find that friendship, they who had never had a friend before. They had stood side by side, their arms raised in victory, and they had not been afraid. The love and the friendship and the strength were in the song that Deborah the Prophetess made for Jael the Kenite.

It was a rich song and its rhythms were the ancient sturdy ones of women's work – of spinning and weaving and pounding and stirring, of bearing down, down against the resistance of the baby's head, breathing into the pain and waiting for the rhythm and the power. Although it was a song of victory, a hymn of triumph to the Lord of Hosts and the army of the north, the men never came to love and use it. Although it was a song of the wheeling stars and the powers of the earth, although it beat to the drum of their daily labour and celebrated the courage of a woman, the wives and mothers were shy of it, nervous at being caught out with that tune on their lips. But the young women, the virgins, and the older women sung it often as they worked. When their fathers and sons and husbands came in from the fields or the hunt asking for water and were tenderly given milk; when they poured the thick goat curds into bowls; when they had occasion to move camp and so pull out the heavy tent-pegs, or to clean and refurbish their menfolk's tools – sickle, mattock, hammer, sword or pruning-hook – they would pause and catch themselves singing a phrase or two from the song that Deborah the Prophetess, a judge in Israel, made for her friend Jael the Kenite, a woman of the tents. Then they would smile and so remember.

Jael fondles the tent-peg, one hand wrapped firmly around it, the other stroking the pointed end caressingly.

Jael tests the weight of the hammer in her hand, resistant, solid, heavy, beautiful.

Jael looks at Sisera asleep, his noble head turned slightly sideways on the pillow she has laid out for him, his hair smoothed back from his forehead – by her, by her.

Her smile is not kind.

Between the thick oiled plaits of his head and the scented silken growth of his beard, his temple glows sweetly in the moonlight. He is a man, a king, bred and fed on royal food. He is the most powerful, the most beautiful man she has ever seen. He is more beautiful than she could have imagined a man could be: even looking at him asleep soothes the dry itching which has come between her and her husband for two years now; she is softened by his beauty, by his easy assumption of power. She melts for him – dark and deep in her belly, and she laughs at herself with a pure pleasure. She is too old for this now she thinks, but she laughs and does not care. Even sleeping he carries his authority with him, the dreams he dreams are royal dreams and Jael laughs in the moonlight.

He had come in to her camp without doubt. He commanded and she obeyed. He had asked for water and she had given him milk – the milk she gave her children once and he was younger than her sons. She had brought him curds in a lordly bowl. The services she had resented rendering to her own men, she rendered to him with delight, with a well-founded sense of rightness. Who would do less or otherwise for such a man? For the first time in her life there is no gap, no dark opening, between service and pleasure – it is seamless now. Before she places the point of the tent-peg against that sweet moon-silver skin she promises herself that she will kiss the spot – a moment of passion and melting joy that she has not felt for years, but which she is about to earn.

First she goes out of the tent and looks around her, filling herself with the moment. Her men have gone to the war; there is an enormous silence in the high desert. It is dark but she can pick out the rough edges of the mountains, the shagged heaps of additional darkness against the dark sky. She can hear the warmth that seeps out from the goat fold and smell the heavy round moon sigh towards its setting. She tastes, sharp on her tongue, the burning stars that wheel above her and the small encampment. She is glad that it is the travelling season, so that their tent and she are solitary. There is no one to share, to steal or to claim this huge night and this beautiful man who are hers now and hers alone. Her skin feels alive; not the agonised night itching of the invisible skin ants which trek their own travels across her thighs, but newly alive, flowing, embracing, reaching, longing. It is cool after the heat of the day and she is cool now after the heat of her own desire. Her laughter breaks the silence.

She is very joyful. She turns back. She moves forward.

Inside the tent she does not hesitate. She stoops and kisses the soft skin as she has promised herself. Then she kneels, not to adore but to ground herself, strong and firm for her strong deed. She is a strong and practical woman; a woman of the tents, who has driven the tent-pegs in to ground far harder than a man's skull.

The familiar weight of the hammer is with her now; the peg is a part of her body. With her first blow she breaks sharp through the skin, penetrates deep in to the bone. And now the point is finding its own way home, its own pathway into the depths of the man.

He groans once, and she has heard that groan before.

She tosses away her own carefulness, joining him in the wild place where the groan once grew sweet and whole. The pounding rhythm, hers this time, not his, her rhythm, her power and long after it is necessary, long after the peg has passed right through his brains and is forcing itself into the sun-baked ground beneath the bedding. Bang. Bang.

Bang, bang, bang. Rhythmical and powerful.

In, and in and in. Deeper, harder. Deeper and harder and the hole in his face opens, stretches out, welcomes each blow.

In and in. The blood and the flesh splash up on to her skin; they flow out over the sheepskin cover; over the pillow, over her hands, her face, her clothes.

She is delighting in her own strength.

In her power.

Bang. Bang. Bang. Deeper and stronger.

Her moment in history.

Her song.

Her story.

Her revenge.

Later she sinks exhausted against the bedplace, lying close to what had once been a noble general, a prince among men; warm against what had been a beautiful and powerful man – until he met her. She sees that with his last reflex he has shat himself; his head is smashed in and his lower body is filthy with spunk and shit. Worn out by her own excitement she giggles: not very regal now, not very manly; and she – she, Jael, a woman too old to bleed, the past-it, dried-out old wife of Heber the Kenite, a simple tent woman and goatherd – she has done this.

She surveys her conquered territory. He is broken and dead. Her best sheets and skins will be unusable, ever again. The elaborate embroidered clothes he wore, the oiled, gold-braided hair, the perfumed beard – all ruined with blood and fragments of bone. Looking at the mess she has another, fiercer, more intense moment of triumph. When her husband returns from the war and sees what she has done, he will be very very frightened, of her, of her.

Deborah the Prophetess had looked at the slaughter on the battlefield beneath Mount Tabor and she had laughed. This was her doing: the broken chariots, the great army of Sisera put to the sword, and the slow mounting chants of victory from the tribes. All her doing – and the Lord's. She, a woman, had called out an army, had appointed Barak its leader, had created a worthy general out of a golden boy. She had been his courage, and the courage of all the army of the northern tribes. Because of her the oppression and the captivity of the people had been ended. It was something to be proud of and she was proud and she had laughed.

But now she stands at the opening to Jael's tent, and she looks inside and her laughter is drowned in a fiercer joy. Suddenly, for the first time in fifty years it does not matter to her that she is an ugly woman. She had wept about it in her youth and grieved it silently through her adult life. Now, though she knows she shed her last blood when the army charged down the hillside into the valley and that now she is dry and finished as woman, she knows too that it does not matter. She is free of that grief. Her words are strong and beautiful instead. And they are true. She had told Barak that the Lord God would deliver Sisera into the hands of a woman. Here was Jael, small, poor, simple, with the blood of Sisera on her hands and a dark mirth silent in her eyes.

Barak, the conqueror, general of the victorious army, the glory of the nation, adulated by his troops, battle-honoured, young, handsome and admired, is very very frightened.

Things have slipped from his control. He does not like it. He does not know what he does not like about it. Something has gone wrong for him.

It is the two women. They are not looking at him. They are looking at each other. They are not old these women, but they are both old enough to be his mother. His mother looks at him, gives him milk when he asks for water. These women look at each other. They have stolen his triumph from him and left him shaken with fear.

The battle itself had never scared him. The Lord God of Armies had fought with him. He, Barak, was a righteous sword of the Lord; he was the defender of the liberties of the people, and the protector of the true and mysterious Name. He was the hand of the Power that drowned the Egyptians, the wielder of the doom prepared for the blasphemers. On the battlefield, he had tasted his own manhood in the rush of the charge from Mount Tabor. He had scented the admiration of his enemies on the strong wind of carnage that encourages a man, that builds him up and reminds him of his birthright. But now, now he has to look at the rough tent standing so mildly by the well side, at the goats and sheep softly, sweetly picking at the sparse mountain grass and he feels sick with his fear. He does not want to have to go back into that tent, to look at that crazy little woman and the bloody mess, the vile remains of another great man and a noble enemy.

Deborah and Jael look at each other. They smile at each other. They are friends. They have both come a long way to find this friendship. It is new and delicate. It is ancient and sturdy. Like a just-born child or an ancestral song. Neither of them has ever had a friend before; not someone to share a joke as deep as this one. They look at the smashed head of Sisera; at the blood-soaked bedding; at the tent-peg still upright in the ground; at the slight sag of each other's stomachs; at the nervous evasions of the boy general. And they smile.

They reach out hands towards each other, unspeaking, oblivious to everything else. Almost shy with excitement they touch each other very gently. The both know their husbands will never want to touch them again. They know who the enemy is. They smile more certainly, and then laugh, breathing in the exhilarating stink of fear that comes to their nostrils.

They walk together out of the tent, their arms round each other, bending gracefully together to avoid the door hangings. They straighten up and look around; and they rejoice because the whole army, the whole victorious, exultant, manic, excited army is silent with fear.

Deborah the Prophetess takes the arm of Jael the Kenite just above her wrist and holds her right hand high for all the men in the army to see. She had told them that the Lord would deliver Sisera into the hand of a woman – let them see that hand; let them see that woman. She had told them that the stars in their courses would fight against Sisera. She had spoken with authority and they must know and see it. Jael is smaller, lighter than Deborah who can hold her friend's clenched fist high without strain and the army sees the victor, the despoiler, the glory of the people, the claimer of the spoils.

Deborah laughs, dark and fierce. Jael laughs, higher, shriller. But the men watch in silence.

What is the source of the joy that lights up these women?

What are the words of the song that they will sing together?

What power drove the hand that drove the nail?

The men have to look at the women. They have to hear the laughter. And they are sick with fear.

On Becoming a Fairy Godmother

~

THEY SAY, 'There is nothing before the Big Bang, just as there is nothing north of the North Pole.'

But here am I, heading up the A68, north of the Wall, in the high wild country between the Tyne and the Border, the dark shoulders of the Cheviots looming beyond the reach of my headlights; heading north through the wind and the dark and the stars. They say there is nothing north of the North Pole, but I am heading north to find out. I am hunting Nothing through the short northern night.

They call it burn-out, but I call it re-entry. It's like space flight – you zoom off and then you go round and round for years and years, orbiting in the vast emptiness, using up your fuel, spinning weightless for half a lifetime. Then there is a sudden pause. You are poised for a moment of stillness. Then you crash back, re-enter the atmosphere, are real again, heavy and solid in the world. The whirling spheres stabilise, the stars calm down, take up their fixed places, float serenely in the sky. I'm not saying it doesn't hurt – that heaviness and humility – but it is not burn-out; it is re-entry.

I was a Child Protection Officer. It is a terrible thing to be. I came too near to the foulness – to the stenching, sulphurous pit. I also came too near my own incompetence, omnipotence, self-righteousness and smug, ugly pride. None the less I was a good Child Protection Officer.

And then I fell in love.

I fell in love with a mother, who was still a child. My princess.

She was a stroppy cow, that young woman, and I loved her for it. Young woman? She was a child, under a spell herself. An evil charm that stopped her doing anything that might be seen to be in her own interest. She hated me. I loved her for it. I'd stand on that hideous cold balcony, ringing the broken bell to her flat, and waiting eagerly for the hot storm of her fury. She'd come to the door, sluttish, in a grubby T-shirt and knickers. She would peer at me with a dark scowl of recognition. I'd look

. . . and see arise
More lovely than the living flowers, the hatred in her eyes . . . .
O you who drain the cup of life, O you who wear the crown,
You never loved a woman's smile as I have loved her frown.

Like that: though certainly not as Chesterton had in mind. If you have never been there then count your blessings, but I will still be sorry for you. She was wonderfully, creatively, totally, bloody-minded.

It wasn't really me she hated, or not entirely. It was the Child Protection Officer, the Social Services that she hated – and who should blame her? We did indeed want to interfere in her life, treat her a child, deprive her of her few pleasures, and tell her we knew better than she did about her own daughter. There was a fierce purity in her though; we could not cow her, frighten her into compliance. She wouldn't, couldn't and certainly didn't take advice from Social Services. She was neither humble nor grateful. We had Mirelle, the child's child, on the 'at risk' register, practically from birth, and rightly probably. We would have had her in care if I hadn't fallen in love.

There was a problem. She wouldn't seek help. She wouldn't keep appointments. She did leave the child alone in the flat. She did shout and rage and scream at her. And at us. She spent too many evenings and too much money in the Ball and Crown, a notoriously sleazy pub, well known to us and to the police. She was vulnerable to both her dealer and her pimp. She had no support network and a difficult background. She was too young. She was unstable. She was a self-harmer, a cutter. This was all true, no question. But I began to think that some of it was laid on for us; that she actually did much better when we left her alone. I knew that she loved the child, incompetently but fiercely. I knew that we frightened her, that she knew we wanted to steal her baby and lock it in a tower. Fear drove her furies and we were not helping. I could not convince myself that we could guarantee anything better for the baby than she was offering. Mirelle would have been a hard-to-place child anyway – special needs bulging all over her, what with the disability and the grim promise of surgery in the future.

I didn't think we could do more than we were doing; I thought we should do less. This was not a popular perspective in my department. We were harried by our own failures, threats and media criticism, mostly deserved. No one was going to let another child slip through our webs, so we spun like spiders on speed

One thing we could do less of, I argued, was listen to the neighbours. Her housing was another problem: the only accommodation we could offer her was in a block designed for the 'independent elderly'. She was surrounded by twelve old ladies who certainly wished well for Mirelle, but they wanted her to be good and quiet and sweet and pretty and gentle and blonde and healthy and virtuous and cute and affectionate and pink and adorable. Mirelle was pretty much none of these things, and every one of the gossiping dozen thought they could magic her into a proper baby, or at the very least do a better job with the child than its mother was doing. They also wished to prove us incompetent. So they nagged at and criticised her. She was not grateful, but obscenely abusive, so they telephoned and nagged at us, and once even got up a petition and said they would go to the local press. Of course they were not going to do that, but they did not have enough excitement in their sad lives so they went on and on and on, in a cackling and competitive chorus until their endless voices drowned out hers.

It went on. There was no crisis, she was not wilfully stupid, but it was not getting any better either. We would not get out of her hair, and she would not cooperate with lice. There were threats, on both sides, and scenes. I was terrified she would hit some junior officer so I made more and more of the calls myself. She did push me once, hard, and it hurt, but luckily there were no observers or witnesses. No one was listening to her and no one in the team was listening to me. Then we had yet another case conference and I lost my temper, just briefly, just long enough for everyone to notice that my famous and much admired calm front was slipping. Someone said I was 'over-involved.' They were right. So I slapped in my resignation.

This caused a gratifying flap. My line manager did not want to lose me. They offered me extra leave and counselling, but I just wept and bitched until they accepted it.

'Burn-out,' they said sadly; and avoided me lest it be infectious. My face burned with a strange shame, even though I did not believe in it. I almost avoided myself.

But then, suddenly, no longer bound to the wheel, I had space in my brain for a cunning plan. I worked my notice. The team needed me, and I needed the time.

At last I went for my final visit to her. It was twenty-four hours before I left the job. I would like to be able to say that the news of my departure caused her a moment of regret, an instant of doubt or sorrow. It did not. Her eyes blazed with a dark malevolent triumph and her wishes for my future were both profane and painful. She stood there, sullen and victorious, and I played my ace.

'By the way, ' I said, and I said it in my prissiest and most sincere social worker voice, 'There's a so-called fortune-teller setting up in the area. We gather she dresses up as some sort of Egyptian character. We cannot approve of this sort of superstition and waste of money. I must earnestly advise you not to go anywhere near her. We would take it quite seriously, now I've warned you. Do you understand me?'

She gave me a glance of perfect contempt, for which I can hardly blame her. Luckily, she was so used to feeling bossed and bullied by us that she did not notice the peculiarity of this particular instruction.

'Don't go to this fortune-teller,' I told her. I ordered her, and could not but admire her mulish antagonistic look.

While she went to get Mirelle, I also slipped ten ten-pound notes into her box of tea bags. I knew she would have no qualms about keeping them and it would not occur to her that a social worker could have done such a generous thing, so it seemed safe enough. I thought she could do with a new and glittery outfit and a free drink next time she went to the Ball and Crown.

Then I left. Later that night, once it was dark, with a scarf over my head I went back to her flat. I slipped a highly elaborate black card, embossed with golden pyramids and hieroglyphs, through her letterbox. It invited her that very Friday to a free introductory tarot reading by the Priestess of Isis-Ra, an initiate of the ancient Wisdom Cult of Osiris, now newly arrived from Nablus in Upper Egypt. I had decided on an Egyptian theme because I needed something that would justify a veil and in any case I thought it would be more fun for her than a dreary old witch with grey hair and a crystal ball.

Twenty-four hours later I was not a Child Protection Officer any more, I was an unemployed, middle-aged woman. None the less I was busy. I bought a black wig with a low fringe; a floaty veil that fitted below my eyes; a good deal of heavy gold-looking jewellery; long black silk gloves; liquid eye-liner – the sort no one has used since the early 70s; and a pack of Tarot cards. I had to go back for a book: it occurred to me that I did have to know something – at least the names of the characters. I borrowed a friend's house. His basement was his studio so it all looked arty and weird enough.

'I hope you know what you're doing,' he said slightly nervously, as I made my preparations. I hoped I did too. I overrode his objections and filled the room with smoke and incense.

Of course she came: nervous, sceptical, bolshy, rude. But also, alive, as I have never seen her before. She had washed, brushed her hair, and despite the piercings actually looked quite pretty. She sat down, giggled and told me haughtily that she didn't believe any of this, of course. She had just come for a laugh.

I made a dark purring sound deep in my throat, raised my gloved hands and made some mystical gestures. I told her in a conjured foreign accent not to worry, the cards spoke more clearly to believers, but I was a true believer and my belief would do for both of us until she was ready to enter into the truths that were timeless.

I asked her if she had any questions, and she said that

was for her to know and me to find out. I quite admired that. So I handed her the pack of cards and told her to shuffle them and wish. Then I took them from her and dealt the first spread. I had sort of adapted my technique from those in the book; I wanted to keep it simple for me and mysterious for her. I was a bit startled when the central card was the High Priestess.

'This is you, your life, your concerns; you are an intelligent, spiritual person, you have a key to secret wisdom and strong emotions, but you can be selfish and overemotional.' This was what it said in the book, and it seemed about right.

I dealt on, laying the cards out in a complex pattern, which I hoped looked meaningful. When I'd finished I turned down the light and we sat in the half dark, illuminated by candles. I muttered about ancient ways, the journey of the soul and the Major Arcana. Next to the Priestess was the Page of Cups.

'Is there a young man in your life?'

She looked properly scornful.

'No, I don't mean a lover – I'll say lover if I mean lover,' I purred. 'Younger than that, much younger. No, perhaps not a man, perhaps a woman, but very young, before there is too much difference. If you weren't so young yourself, I would think it was your child, a girl child?'

'Yeah, well,' she glowed a little, either because I thought her young or because I had identified the baby.

I made circles with my palms over the cards I was claiming for the mother and child, then laid my mystical, gloved index fingers on the cards around them, one by one, stroking them slightly. 'There is something very special about this child,' I said.

Like a flame of pure joy, she lit up. 'I don't need you to tell me that,' she said. 'Mirelle is fabulous, she's just great. I love her to bits.'

'She is your candle in the dark.' I shoved one of the candles towards her and she picked it up and held it quite gently. I pushed on, relieved and emboldened, pleased both by the obvious sincerity and by my own acumen.

'The cups, the cups suggest . . . does, does your child have something wrong with her hands? Perhaps just one hand?'

She was less surprised than I had expected. Clearly this enhanced my authority, but it did not startle her. It dawned on me that whatever she had said when she arrived, she was in fact the believer, not me.

'Yeah,' said, looking sad, 'It's all fucked, like weird. I hate it . . . it scares me, because, like, it might be my fault.'

My heart stopped. Oh shit, I thought, what am I going to do if she tells me she inflicted that on the child.

'Like when I fell for her, right when I first guessed, I sort of lost it there, and I like cut up my own arms. And I . . . like when I saw hers I got to thinking that perhaps that was what did it to her. The doctor says no, no, just one of them things, but you know they're all plonkers, what do they know? That's why I don't do it any more, cut I mean, it's not right when you've got a kid. Sometimes I have to sort of run out the house, or get smashed or away on something, but I don't cut. It'd feel like cutting her, somehow.'

Child protection. We hadn't known any of this. We had thought she was still self-abusing; we thought she 'lacked insight' and concern and effort. Apart from anything else I had never heard her say so much, so many words all at the same time, never. She looked eagerly at the cards and at me to go on.

I told her that the baby was in danger. That there were cosmic plots afoot; forces that wanted to steal Mirelle, kidnap her, keep her, because the child was very precious and had special, though unspecified, powers. But she was the High Priestess, she had the knowledge. She had been sent to guard Mirelle, to thwart the dark forces. She must never, never leave the child on its own. There might, I hinted, be adventures and dramas to come. I issued dire, though vague, warnings. I did not mention Quality of Care. I said they were complicated conspiracies, powers in league with one another. I outlined a description of her pimp, nothing definite enough for her to be sure. I left her dealer and my successor out of it. Then I turned my attention to the final card I had laid out – I touched it. I started my hand shaking, I moaned slightly and collapsed forward, my head on the table, my hair across the spread.

'I'm sorry,' I gasped, rocking backwards and forwards in my distress, 'I can't go on. It is too strong; it's all too powerful. You are a strong women, with a strong soul. The spirits are too weighty now. I haven't given you the full reading, but I cannot go on tonight. Can you come back? Can you come back next week and we will try again, try to go further?'

Well of course she came back. Anyone would after that. Despite the growing concern of my friend she came weekly, on Friday evenings. I would deal the spreads and we would examine them. The cards described her pimp in detail and told her how to outwit him. The cards exposed the evil machinations and sinister collaborations between her social worker and her dealer; both were bond slaves of the dark powers, hunting for Mirelle. It was her duty to trick them – for example to pretend compliance, co-operation and civility.

The cards even suggested places she might look for allies. The cards indicated the best of the old neighbours as a white force, one who could be trusted. The honoured old lady was courted, charmed, cut out from the herd and transformed by magic into a surrogate grandmother and babysitter. The cards pointed a mystic way for her to a better GP, to the dentist, to healthier diet, to exercise.

I told her nothing in my Isis-Ra incarnation that I had not told her in my Child Protection Officer manifestation – except of course about the interfering schemes of my old department, and I should have told her that from the start. She was a child, you see, a child who needed stories and magic to grow up on. The only thing I would never talk about was 'the tall dark stranger', her prince – I could not bear it.

In six months she was in Access to Higher Education classes. She learned enough maths to swindle her dealer, and enough law to dump her pimp and look after her own earnings. Then she went on to photography and IT. My erstwhile colleagues were so bloody pleased with themselves that it made me sick – as though she had done nothing, nothing to put her life together and guard her child from them. As though they were knights on stupid white chargers who had rescued her.

Then they took Mirelle off the register, and I was free. Cackling, worrying my friends, jobless, slightly mad, but free. I thought she would be sad when I said goodbye this second time, but she wasn't really. I mean, she said thank you and everything, but you could see she was moving on, growing up, getting a life.

Suddenly that was fine by me. There was a whole shining new world to explore. I decided, one long summer evening, that I would go north, up there somewhere where the days were longer, where the evenings stretched out long pale hands to greet the following morning.

So here I am, heading up the A68, north of the Wall, in the high wild country between the Tyne and the Border, the dark shoulders of the Cheviots looming beyond the reach of my headlights; heading north through the wind and the dark and the stars. I left London this morning and I've been driving all day, not fast, not by motorways, but steadily, steadily northwards. Last night, the last thing I did before escaping, I pulled a scarf over my head and sneaked round to her flat one last time. I wanted to deliver an unsuitable present. I know it will baffle her, she won't get it, or she may think it is for Mirelle, and she will never know it is from me – neither of those mes.

It's a joke, a story, that I wrote for her, my woman-child.

THE FAIRY GODMOTHER COMES OUT

Menopause makes a Fairy Godmother grumpy and disloyal. Since we have no bodies and live only in your minds, our hormones run amok and cannot be tamed by HRT. *This story may be treacherous, I may be breaking faith with my sorority, but my duty and my love have always been to my little girls, and I come and go between the worlds, according to my own whim.*

Now you have stopped believing in me, it is time to break the silence.

Now you think you have escaped into a world of hygiene, disposable nappies and convenience food, it is time to come clean.

So here is a story that you need to know.

Once upon a time, or twice, or a thousandth upon a time, a baby girl is born and there is much rejoicing.

Her parents, be they cottagers or kings, royalty or ragamuffins, invite the fairies to her naming feast and she is given magic gifts. The gifts are given secretly in vellum envelopes, scented with lavender and sealed with beeswax, and they must be guarded with care. No one knows what these gifts are or will be and by tradition we fairies never tell.

But I am going to tell. I'm going to hand over the secret files. Menopause may have tattered my tulle and frayed my furbelows, but I can still make a silk purse out of a sow's ear (that being the nature of magic), and offer a free lunch to anyone I choose. In the envelope is a tiny mirror, and each girl child will one day look in the mirror and it will tell her which part in the fairy story she is going to play. Because, regardless of all the modern icing on the old cake, regardless of women's rights and post-modernity, you still have to play one role or another in the old tales. The stories were our original gift to you and the fairy world cannot take back its gifts. Luckily however we can transform them and fairies are more artful than you think. And recently we have updated the definitions, so that, once again, you can know what to do with your mirrors, and recognise yourself and all your friends.

For example:

THE POSTMODERNIST PRINCESS

The princess is a spoiled brat who redeems herself through style. A princess is self-ironic – but only because this protects her from revolutionary or republican attack. Obviously therefore a princess has to be beautiful: prettiness is simply not enough.

The Princess is kindly towards her subjects: in childhood her subjects are usually her parents, although they can include both older and younger brothers. On the whole the Princess does not get along with sisters. (A household with two Princesses in it is in deep trouble, but luckily this does not happen very often.) The Princess knows from very early in her life that it is only by a stroke of wicked bad luck that she is in this household at all: she ought truly to be living in a palace. She knows this is not the fault of the woodcutter and his wife who are both her parents and her devotees, and so she is kindly towards them.

The Princess is a people-pleaser. Particularly she likes to have many grown-ups around her, who adore her – teachers, grandmothers and (once she is an adolescent) glamorous-type gay men who are gratified by the surprise that they see on the faces of their peers when they arrive somewhere with a Princess in tow. She naturally thinks that they are in tow and this leads to mutual satisfaction.

The Princess cannot pass a mirror – even a plate glass window or the eyes of another human being – without glancing in to check that she is still the fairest one of all. This is either a deep vanity or a deep fear. Or both.

The Princess was put under a curse, at her christening, by a wicked old witch. The curse can take various forms (so can the christening) but it leads to a belief that she can make choices – that there is no essential gap between choice and its fulfilment, except the malice of others. This erroneous faith leads to intense disappointment, which is sad, and frustration. It can lead to hundred-year-long naps, entombment in glass coffins, or having to wear rags while less lovely and deserving women get to go to the ball. It is more or less impossible for the Princess to accept that the knight in white armour, the handsome prince, has zits. She is necessarily a snob (although this too can take various forms.)

The Princess knows that diamonds are a girl's best friend. And that she ought to have lots of them.

The Princess has a wonderful cleavage, deep and soft.

Even a Princess who has no bosom, who is – as even princesses can be in this decadent and demotic generation – flat-chested, still manages to have a cleavage. This is a royal mystery.

The Princess likes to sleep on linen sheets and can be kept awake all night by a pea, which irritates her not just because she can feel its sharp edges pressing her lily-white skin all night, but because it IS *a pea, and what Princess wants to be reminded of the body's need for green vegetables?*

For example:

CONTEMPORARY WITCHES

Witches are not necessarily old; witches nowadays are usually teenagers. In fact, almost all teenage girls are witches. However, the most powerful witches are those who maintain their magical skills into adulthood.

Pregnancy is the best cure (if cure be desirable) for witchcraft. The baby will tame the mother so that the mother will tame the father so the father will tame the gods. It is in the national interest, therefore, to promote childbearing and the nuclear family. It is also, obviously, in the interests of organised religion to promote families – and indeed to destroy witches.

Every witch fears fire. It would be foolish not to.

All witches have strong creative imaginations: they need them. Since it is not actually possible to be empowered by pagan fertility cults, nor to cast a murrain on your neighbour's cows (even assuming in our post-industrial conurbations that your neighbour has any cows), nor to have sex with the Devil (who hates bodies and therefore hates sex), nor to build houses on chicken's feet or out of chocolate biscuits, nor, in fact, to fly, it is essential to be able to believe that all these things are possible. Witches are therefore playful, energetic, witty and take responsibility for what they do. This may explain why witches so often lose their power when they become grown-ups: very few grown-ups are playful, energetic, witty or take responsibility for what they do.

Most contemporary witches are in strong and effective denial. This has been one of the great successes of the so-called Enlightenment. It is one major reason why oppressive governments and oppressive churches have been prepared to tolerate Enlightenment thinking. A few ideas about individual human rights, however inconvenient, are a small price to pay for persuading women that all witches are bad and also don't exist.

All witches are women. All witches are feminists. (Unfortunately not all feminists are witches.) Lots of people are frightened of witches. Since they do not know which women are witches lots of people are frightened of women. They should be.

Witches are glamorous. Glamour is what witches are and what their power is. There is an element of excitement and an element of deceit in all glamour.

This is crucial. Witches are neither good nor bad. They are powerful.

For example . . .

. . . but no. Think about it. Think about the girl child growing up. Do you recognise her here?

I could fill in the whole sociology – the wicked stepmother, the ice queen, the little mermaid, the faithful nurse, the ugly stepsister. But I, I am the fairy godmother, and I come and go between the worlds, according to my own whim. I have no obligations, only gifts. My generosity is chancy – you cannot call or re-call me, I cannot be relied on. I have things to do and stories to be in that you know nothing about. I'm off now about my own business. You have to do some of the work yourselves.

Believe me, believe me at your peril. The old stories do not lie. They omit and contort and deceive, but they do not lie. If you refuse one part you will have to play another.

But I'll tell you one more thing before I go. That mirror. Each girl child will one day look in her mirror and will know which part in the fairy story she is going to play. What we have kept quiet about for all these years is that when you look in that mirror, you – you and no one else – choose who you see.

I'm away off now about my own business. All day I've been driving; but I still don't want to stop. I want to go further, still further, further out, further in, further up, further down, further on . . . I will probably drive all night. They call it burn-out, but I call it re-entry. They say there is nothing North of the North Pole, and I'm going to take a look.

See you around.

Helen of Troy's Aerobics Class

~

STEP TOUCH SWING. Step touch swing. Arms well up now, above their shoulders.

They work hard. Helen forces the drummer on with a sharp look; and the drum beat forces them all through the long repetitions.

Hop scotch high arms and re-peat.
Hop scotch high arms and re-peat.
Kick away for-ward. And twist back.
Kick away forward and twist back.

They are all beginning to sweat now. A glow on most foreheads and under their arms.

Double scoop, right, double scoop left. Jump. Clap. Turn.

Is this the face that launched a thousand ships? She asks herself crossly, reaching up with a perfectly manicured hand to wipe her upper lip. For a moment she doubts it . . . two three four. The eunuch watches her closely now. He knows his job. He must stop before she does, but only when she is ready to.

Her will drives them into one more sequence. Squat.

Jump. Stretch . . . two three four. Squat. Jump. Stretch. Squat. Jump. Stretch.

And relax. The eunuch continues to beat the rhythm on the small hand drum, but more softly as the women take a break – all of them, their legs slightly apart and their torsos hanging forward. Helen's hair, unbound this morning with only a narrow fillet holding it off her face, brushes the floor in front of her. She notes that it is getting ragged at the bottom, scraggly rats' tails. It is thinning out, weakening, drying; perhaps she should rinse it in cream. The colour is good though, earlier in the bright sunshine outside she had been aware of a possible harshness, a slightly strident shade, but now in the cool tower room it looked good – still the pure white-blonde it had always been. Perhaps she should cut it short, start a new fashion; every woman with their hair bobbed like Amazons to celebrate the heroism of their princes. No. That might make people think of Penthesilea, the Amazon Queen; even Helen had to admit she was rather magnificent, beautiful even, if you liked that mannish type. Odd how some men seemed to. No, long hair was more . . . more Helen really. But she might style it more elaborately, carefully pinned plaits and jewelled combs. Free-flowing was a bit undignified perhaps – and she could let it down slowly, carefully in her bedroom, in the candle light where the thinning would not show, and Paris would be weakened, thrilled, aghast, grateful, quivering at the slow graceful movement and the silvery fall of hair.

She straightens up and sees with annoyance that Cassandra has drifted into the room and is standing by the window looking out at the Greek camp on the plain below. Beyond the camp is the sea, sparkling in the sunshine.

Cassandra says, 'If you stand here They can see you.'

Helen is irritated. She knows perfectly well that if you stand in that window embrasure, any of the Greeks who want to can see you. Indeed she often does stand just there so that they will see her and will remember again why they left wives, lovers, mothers and daughters, why they have been camped in discomfort for so long.

'A cat may look at a queen,' she says haughtily, but she glides over to the window, practising her already perfect sinuous movements, and joins her sister-in-law. Cassandra waves like a child at a Greek soldier who happens to be looking up. Cassandra is quite mad, as everyone knows, and is as likely to wave and smile at the enemy as she is to fall asleep in the middle of a formal banquet or try to take all her clothes off because she is feeling warm. Or to shriek and wail and scratch her face, if the mood is on her.

Helen does not present herself to the gaze of the Greeks as blatantly as Cassandra does, but she looks out as eagerly.

'Who's that?' Cassandra points. 'He's very sexy.'

'My husband,' says Helen shortly. Since Cassandra asks the same questions over and over again, Helen has answered this one several times a week for months and years on end. To herself she thinks that Menelaus, her husband, does not look terribly sexy any more; his hair is speckled silver-grey and he has put on weight.

'And you left him for my brother!' There is something very unattractive in Cassandra's amazement.

Helen wants to say that Cassandra's brother, her lover and Prince of Troy is far better in bed than Menelaus ever was, respectful and grateful. And he is young and lovely. Young, blessed by Aphrodite, and crazy about her. Menelaus was not crazy about her. He had loved her because she was his wife and had been his wife for a long, long time. Paris, on the other hand, was young, eager, and could have chosen any woman. The Gods had promised him the most beautiful woman in the world and, even though she was older than his mother, he had chosen her. His gift from the Gods. On her fiftieth birthday she had run away with him, because in the mirror of his dark eyes she could see herself as the most beautiful woman in the world – the one worth Troy destroyed and the Aegean coast turned into a mausoleum for the heroes of Greece who will never more go home. And because Paris did not know it was her fiftieth birthday – and Menelaus would have drunk her health, teasingly, laughing, at the banquet that evening, and she would have seen Paris startled and doubting. But she does not say these things. Cassandra would not understand – her innocence would shrink, she would be hurt and confused. There is a tenderness in Helen, practised and nurtured but real; there were things no one says to Cassandra because she is crazed, her world broken somehow from within, and her frailty calls out for protection.

'Who's that then?' Cassandra was still looking out the window.

Helen follows her gaze and then glances away.

'Come on, girls,' she calls, 'back to work.' She tries never to think about Odysseus, who had always hated her. Helen is very much aware that if she thinks about things she does not like she tends to scowl, and scowling will wrinkle her forehead, and wrinkles will mar her perfection. She is the most beautiful woman in the world and she has an obligation to maintain her beauty, or else there will be no sense in all of this. It is not vanity, but duty.

The drum beat picks up. Cassandra stays by the window, but Helen rallies the rest and they begin again.

'Sequence three,' she calls, 'Skip turns with punching arms.' The older women look weary, and the younger ones bored. They all try to disguise their feelings. Helen's will pushes them into the Half Jacks and the Grapevines with Arm Circles . . . two three four.

Box step with high arms. Wide. Wide. Three four. And again.

Flat back. Head high. Kick two three four; kick away three four.

For at least an hour. Every day. And it works.

It works. It has to work.

She is nearly sixty and her stomach is as smooth and flat as a teenager's. Her arms are firm, no hanging dewlaps, no softness, no giving in to the ever demanding forces of gravity. Helen feels herself blushing and skips her legs with even greater zeal. She will never again mount her lover and, enthroned above his golden belly, look down and laugh into his eyes. A few months ago she had dropped a ring on the floor and crawling to find it had found herself looking into the polished surface of Paris's shield – which should not have been on the floor of her bedroom. It was his fault. She had seen how the flesh along her jawline slopped forward; how the skin came away from her cheekbones and dropped. There were no exercises for those muscles, no crafty trussing and manoeuvring. Now, when they made love, she would lie beneath him, so that gravity pulled the weight of her face backwards, firming her cheeks and smoothing her long neck. There is a price to be paid.

The price is growing higher. She prefers evenings now, the soft glow of candles to the bright cruel sun. She prefers the dark and the misty dawn. And, she has to face it, she does not believe in fooling herself, Paris approaching thirty is not the same as that glorious teenager, adoring, crumpled with passion, with love, with devil-daring and the all-for-love-and-the-world-well-lost bravado of youth. Spoiled, he had been spoiled rotten from childhood on, and it shows now in softness, in the beginning of pudginess. This was not good enough. When Troy falls, and Troy would fall, she will need Paris to be either beautiful or dead; but he was becoming both plump and cowardly.

They are all lying on their woven mats now, a dozen pairs of legs raised high, twenty-four ankles inscribing circles in the air. Half the women in the room are young enough to be her daughters. She has a daughter, back in Sparta. When she left Hermione had still been a child, now . . . Helen experiences a tremor of terror at the thought of a young and lovely version of herself, free, unblemished, ready. The gossip, for even in the besieged city gossip flows as readily as water, says Hermione loves her cousin Orestes, Agamemnon's oldest boy. Agamemnon had been Helen's suitor once, and had had to make do with her sister, Clytemnestra. Helen smiles, banishing the thought of her daughter.

She concentrates on keeping her arms flat, her spine long against the floor. She does not want to have a lovely grown-up daughter. The poets say that each year Hera, queen of heaven, goes to bathe in the fountain of Canathus, and the enchanted waters restore her virginity, her inviolate pristine triumphant youth. Helen feels envious. It wasn't fair. Hera hated her, was jealous of her, would certainly never allow Helen access to that magical spring. What bliss it would be. She pulls herself together firmly, makes a renewed act of will, points her toes upwards. She is not nearly sixty, she tells herself, she is Helen, blessed by the Gods, and twenty-four forever. She works her ankles with renewed enthusiasm, watching her legs from below with simple pleasure because they are terrific legs.

A shadow falls across her. It is Cassandra, wandering from the window.

'Look Helen,' she says, 'how white your legs are.' She touches one of Helen's feet, then holds it in her little dry hand for a moment. 'It's like a dancing swan.' Helen cannot be sure, from this angle, how knowing Cassandra's childlike smile is.

The swan. The great swooping power of the swan. Zeus came as a swan for her conception, in the huge flurry of white strength, there in the moment that she dreams of. Her mother, Leda, had not deserved such power, such whiteness. It cannot have been for Leda that the swan came. The swan's huge desire was for the creation of Helen. Helen insists on that, argues herself into agreement with that. Leda had been nothing: a cipher, a pawn in the God's game. Zeus lusted here, there and everywhere, there was nothing special about Leda, nothing to move a God. It was Helen whom Zeus had desired. For Helen, Zeus had come in that white fall by the river bank, had come in glory to bring her into being. Her father, the God of Gods, Lord of Olympus, paternal for once, protective, attentive, kind. It was she, Helen, whom Zeus loved and cherished.

She feels the pressure of Cassandra's hand, firm. They say Apollo once fancied Cassandra. But Zeus comes as the swan, comes as strength and beauty and power. She wriggles her foot free of Cassandra's hold and jumps up. Cassandra is mad and has let herself go. She could have been quite an attractive woman, Helen thinks looking at her, but she was not willing to make the effort. Helen is willing. She looks at the eunuch who has been startled by this change in the routine. He knows his job however and takes the drum rhythm forward with her, forcing all the other women off their backs and on to their feet.

'Sequence one again,' she commands. 'Step touch swing. Step touch swing and . . . Box Step with monkey arms. One, two, three, four.'

Cassandra backs off, looking sly, and retires to the window again, whence she waves at more Greeks.

Cheap, thinks Helen. She is angry now. She will not be angry. Anger is not lovely. Serenity is lovely. Helen makes herself serene. They start an Alternate Squat and Skip routine. Up up up up. Knees up, up, up to our chins. Now, heads back, arms out, clap, two, three, four. Helen can feel her breasts joggling. She does not want them to stretch. Ugly, sagging. A giveaway, stretched breasts would be, but no one will see. She and Paris will do it in the dark. Put out the candles, dear heart, she will say. Let me love you by moonlight. He is a moon calf anyway. She can feel her irritation and thinks at once and firmly about something else.

The best time had been the year before she married.

Sparta, the golden kingdom, the kingdom of joy. She and her sister and their cousin Penelope . . . but she will not think about Penelope: Odysseus had spoiled it all, had ruined the glories of that summer, had broken ranks, had abandoned the everlasting and insatiable courtship of Helen and fallen in love with her mousy cousin. She will not think about Penelope. All this war, all this trouble and her own anxieties, they are all Penelope's fault. She will not think about Penelope.

She will think about her *succès fou*; her season of love. When all the heroes of Greece left their home cities, deserted their duties, abandoned their families and flocked to Sparta to try and win the lovely Helen in marriage. They hunted and picnicked and danced; they rode and raced and wrestled; they ate and played and sang. Every man had wanted her and every woman had hated her.

She has not forgotten the name of a single suitor. Now those names become the drum rhythm to which she does her exercises:

Antilochos, son of Nestor

Diomedes

Megas

Ajax

Achilles

Patroclus

Menelaus

Agamemnon

Ascalpus and Iamus, sons of the God of War

Odysseus . . . but she will not think about him, because he has always hated her and will be her undoing yet.

Thapius. Mnesthius, Polyxenes . . .

She grows bored with her list . . . 'Come on,' she urges, 'put some strength into it. Kick away forward and twist back.' . . . All the heroes of her generation had adored her. More than half of them are out there on the sea plain, their ships dragged up, their wives and cities deserted, still fighting and competing for her, for Helen, though she is nearly sixty and fears the harsh light of midday.

It is just not possible for other women to understand the difficulties and responsibilities of being so beautiful. If you pay too much attention to anyone, the others will be jealous. Women will be mean to you, giggle about you, drop into uneasy silences when you enter a room. Even her parents had got nervous, had grudged her that long hot summer by the sea. They should have been delighted. They should have been proud. They should not have got so nervous, should not have ordered her to calm down, to ease up. Jealous. Her mother had been jealous because she was so beautiful, because every man had desired her, because even her father . . . but, no, of course he was not her father. It was all right. Zeus Lord of Lords and King of Olympus was her father. They should not forget that. It was not her fault she was so beautiful.

She had been so happy then. And Menelaus had been so thrilled and . . . and then she had married him and it was all over.

He had been a good husband, but . . . Well, who could have endured having all the others trek off to their own homes and find themselves other wives quite as satisfactory to them, and settle down and come on visits and greet her with an old and amused affection, remembering that summer as diversion, while for her it had been her life? And they would talk about their households and their children, their sons, as though they had entirely forgotten that one glorious summer they had been honoured to rise before dawn and go out to gather wild flowers, so that she could walk on scented petals all the way from the women's quarters to the great hall.

And when she had left Sparta, renewed and revivified in the eyes of Paris, and Menelaus had recalled them all to their ancient vow – some of them had not wanted to come. Some of them had not wanted to leave their cosy middle-aged homes and sail to Troy to rescue her.

Odysseus had feigned madness and Achilles disguised himself as a woman, shamed himself so rather than delight in her summons for aid.

Paris had been all of them for her; had been all her admirers, lovers, suitors reborn. Her courageous adventure into his arms had made the whole world see her afresh and value her beauty with their lives.

They are all flagging now, arms less keen and claps less sharp. She is tempted to make them go on, to teach them the price. But her own underarms are feeling wet. She lets them all lie to do their cool-down stretches. She feels a sort of relief.

When Troy falls and they take her back and count their dead, she has to have been worth it, or there is nothing. They have to look at her and say 'Of course. Of course it is right that brave men died here, for in Helen's loveliness is the honour of all Greece; and every man who would not throw away the gifts of all the Gods for one smile from her peerless lips is a blind fool.' They have to go home to their wives a little sorry; they have to go home knowing that she was a cause beyond causes, and that the Gods, who love wisdom, will love even more the folly men commit for Helen's sake.

So she exercises daily. She bathes in goat's milk. She never smiles too freely, or thinks about things that might upset her. She never walks out in the garish sun. But sometimes in the evenings, she will stroll along the ramparts, a misty veil round her shoulders so that the warriors in the Greek camp will see her and draw inspiration from the sight. The soldiers of Troy, within their besieged city, will see her too and be willing to die rather than yield up their diadem, their immortality, their pearl.

The women cross their left legs over their bent right knees. Helen leads them into their Waist Crunches, their Spine and Abdominal Stretches. Her inner thighs need very little toning. She is nearly perfect, but she runs no risks. It would be wicked to let herself go.

'Go for the burn,' says Cassandra sardonically as she drifts away from the room.

Troy will burn for Helen.

This is the face that launched a thousand ships

And burned the topless towers of Ilium.

It is just a face; and one best loved by its owner, cherished more tenderly than her husband cherishes his kingdom or her lover cherishes his family honour. It is real, that beauty. It will be the cause of many good men's deaths. Later when she has bathed she will dress herself in a simple white robe and a diaphanous cloak and will walk through the city to sit with the old king, who will look at her and dote, who will forgive his foolish son, her foolish lover, anything and everything because he has brought this treasure to Troy.

No one quite knows how she does it. She is nearly sixty years old, and occasionally looks tired and worn. Then, ah then, she will smile, or glide across a room, or lift an eyebrow, or just turn her head, and every man who sees her thinks 'Yes.' Thinks, 'Yes I will die for her.' Thinks of a white swan swooping down in power beside a blue river and envies Paris. Thinks, 'Yes I am blessed, fortunate to have seen her passing.' Thinks, 'Yes she is worth a thousand ships, a hundred thousand men who will never go home and all the bright flames and dead ash of Troy.'

It is very hard work for her though.

Choosing Paradise

Just before we felt the first tremor, in a single
moment at the edge of town [Watsonville,
California] a million apples had fallen to the ground
simultaneously. They made a tiny earth tremor of
their own, it showed up on the seismographs,
although we did not notice
it at the time. One million apples: there have
not been one million days in the two millennia
since the beginning of the Common Era.
That is one hell of a lot of apples.

Newspaper report. 1989 earthquake, California, USA

THEY HAD PLANTED AN ORCHARD, on a long gentle slope beneath the mountain. Above it the rocks rose steeply, protecting the spring blossom from the vicious frosted winds. Below it, levelling out, were the vegetable and grain fields before the land dropped away into rolling valleys, with copses of great trees, green at noon and blue grey in the evening mists. When the air was especially clear, far out behind the green lands, they could just see the desert, shimmering, dancing, stretching to the horizon.

It had not been easy establishing the orchard. When drifting eastward, uncertain and unsettled, they had first come upon the place it had been the lower farmland that had held their attention – the rich pink soil and the steady flow of the river. They had settled there, learned to milk the cow from watching their children on her breast; learned to till the rosy earth and plant and weed and tend. Only later had they turned their energies to the higher ground, heaving rocks and stones through the hot sweaty summer, hacking through thorns and thistles. They had searched out and gathered in the little trees and planted them deep. They had waited, for an orchard takes a long time to grow, longer even than a child: but the children were grown now, the boys taller than their father and stronger, and the orchard was grown too.

It was an orderly place of frothy blossom and red-gold harvest. They had cherries and almonds and olives and figs. Pears, tangerines, grapes and quinces. Fat sharp gooseberries and red currants, white currants and black currants. Mulberries, loganberries and a great walnut tree with a smooth grey trunk and fingering leaves. They had plums and pomegranates and apples. He had not wanted apples, but she loved them; they were easy to bring to fruit and the warm smell of them contrasted so delightfully with the juicy firmness against her teeth. She had insisted on apples.

She liked the orchard and the farmstead and mostly she stayed there and worked through the long busy days, while he and their lovely sons went out, ploughed the fields below, shepherded the flocks and hunted for venison, rabbit and quail. They were not happy exactly, they could never be happy again, but resigned and, with the resignation, content.

Like now. The hard day's work was ended and she sat in the flowery grass under the shade of her fruit trees and watched a jaguar, sand-gold and black-spotted, his heavy tail languorous, roll in the bluebells beside the stream. The fruit was coming to ripeness, hanging waiting, and soon the men would come home and they would have their harvest.

There. Now. Here. Then. Then. Then there was a moment, a shiver, a distortion, a movement of perfect stillness, the sound of silence. The still moment before, well known to epileptics and to those sitting at the epicentre of where there is about to be an earthquake and who are paying attention.

Eve was good at paying attention. She felt the stillness, the shiver, the distortion. In that single moment a million apples fell. She felt a warm vibration, rounder than rain, softer than hail, as the firm apples hit the ground. Before she could cry out the earth began to move. To dance perhaps. And in the tumbling dancing, breaking craziness of the world she saw again, bright and slitty, the eager eyes of the serpent, most subtle of all the wild creatures, the eyes of everlasting sarcasm, glittering and mocking.

This is the first earthquake. This is the first time the slow grinding tectonic plates have shoved into each other, shunted, wedged and shifted so that deep down below the orchard there is a sudden slippage, and the pressure of fire from below and the pressure of the weighty rock above struggle for their equilibrium and the world judders, twists and falls inwards against itself. This has never happened before. Before, in Eden, the world had spun smoothly on its vertical axis, the magnetic lines running true north and south, from pole to pole. It was when Eve bit the apple, when she broke the first and only law and bit the apple, that the universe rebounded in horror, shocked, shaken to its core. The single smooth plate on which it was built cracked, lines running outwards from the centre, crazing. The destabilised world shook, wobbled, tottered and tipped out of true, slipped over a few degrees, 23½ degrees – and then there was Weather, seasons, zones, volcanoes, lightning bolts. Earthquakes. It took its time. One crack in the perfect creation and it crizzled outwards forever, slowly but surely the flaws in the fabric, the rents and rips and irregularities develop, and the consequences form themselves into events. This is the first earthquake.

It stopped. The sun came out again. The earth calmed, lay down and slept again, as though it had never moved. Below her in the fields the maize heads, swelling gold, were ending some wild dance, soothing back to their usual gentle waves. There was a strange silence before the birds began to chirp tentatively, then start to sing. The fallen fruit littered the grass around her, in piles, heaps, mounds, bruised and bleeding thick discoloured juice. It had been real, not a dream.

She did not know what was happening. She only knew that everything she had ever known had been grounded in the fact that the world was established on firm foundations, solid beneath her feet. It did not dance and bound. It did not rock and roll. Pitch and toss. Now it was not firm any more, not strong and still: it had bucked like a colt, leapt like a stag. Everything has changed.

She has changed.

Slowly she clambers to her feet, standing in the pulpy piles of wasted apples and she examines herself, because she knows that she has changed. She has never seen herself in a mirror, except in the eyes of her man; and she is more than old enough to know that there is nothing stable, established, grounded or well-founded in any image of a woman in the eyes of a man. She knows herself by her body. Through her fingers that feel her own curves and know that they have softened, dropped, ripened over the long years since she woke in the gaze of his eyes. Through breasts that pull downwards, ache a little when she runs. Through hair that no longer flows like a stream, but is dryer, more brittle on her head, and sparser between her legs. Through the silvery purple marks where the children had stretched her skin in their birthing. These are changes. Something else has changed now.

There, in the dappled sun under her apple trees, she explores the new world of herself – the exterior and the interior until she has rediscovered herself in this new place. Then she knows. The bleeding has stopped. Not just stopped for now, the way it does, but stopped forever. Something that has moved in a pulsing circle through each moon's growing and dying, something that is deep inside her, is stilled, calmed, gone. The frightening bleeding from between her legs has stopped, gone away, ceased, finished, ended. Deep inside her something has changed, grown, moved forward, altered and the bleeding has stopped.

This is the change. Her heart is beating, thumping with excitement, and she tries to calm herself down. It is too much joy, more than they had ever hoped for. She wants Adam to come so that she can tell him. She thinks of Adam with pleasure. Then quickly she takes pleasure in the warm affection of her thought. Because before when she had thought of Adam her stomach would clench, buzz within her, and her desire would bend her towards him unable to escape, long for him greedily, want to absorb him, take him in to her, press him closer and embrace him inside her. Now, in her excitement, she notices that she can think of him suddenly without excitement. This is part of the change.

She checks her body again. She is not having a child. She has not had a child for a long time now; she has had enough children, she has done that. There is no child now, no little knot at the base of her belly, no tenderness in her breasts, no queasiness in her mouth, no swelling in her ankles.

The bleeding has stopped. The curse is lifted.

They can go back. They can go home.

Once upon a time they had lived in a garden.

The Garden of Eden. Paradise. Not farm nor field, not orchard nor pasture. Garden – which means that beauty comes first, not a long laboured-for second, trailing in after husbandry, food, need, life. In their garden the ground was blessed not cursed and gave sweetness to them without their labour. In their garden the trees bent down to feed them and they were without need: food and drink and sleep and sex and solitude and company were for delight and they knew no shame. And like the trees there, she had been smooth and lovely, made for loveliness not usefulness. She had been juicy, fruitful, lovely. Young and innocent. Happy.

Now, in the aftermath of the earthquake, she thinks about their garden and she knows that resignation is a poor contemptible thing and that contentment is not sufficient. She knows she desires joy. She is happy, flooded with unaccustomed, half-forgotten joy, because the bleeding has stopped. The curse is lifted and she can go home.

She leaves the orchard, through the thicket fence they have protected it with, and turns to the West, walking towards the setting sunset, towards Paradise. She does not wait for Adam, for he may be gone many days, he may be any place, and perhaps he too will have a way of knowing that the dark times are over, that the curse is lifted and that they are forgiven, restored. She thinks perhaps she will meet him near the gate, or that he will come to her there, young, unscarred, golden. Then she does not think of him at all, but only of going home.

It is not that far. They had not travelled very far; just over the hill so they could no longer see the wall of their garden. Now, as she walks home, she sheds her clothes, like an apple tree sheds its blossom. She likes the feel of herself walking naked across the shoulder of the hill and looking down into the valley where she has not been for so many years. The evening breeze caresses her. She had forgotten how good it felt to walk in a soft breeze, naked and unashamed.

She almost runs down the long slope on the other side of the hill, quickening her pace, laughter welling up in her as she slips and skids where the slope becomes steeper. At the bottom she wades across the small river. The water comes up against her thighs and creams there where her legs dam its onward rush to the sea. She slips; her toes, invisible in the fast brown water, brace against the smooth stony bottom. Then with a squeal of delight she surrenders, falling forward into the water, accepting the shock of coldness against her naked belly, splashing and giggling. She feels clean, washed pure and childlike again.

She scrambles out on the far bank, still laughing, fresh and sparkling and turns downstream for the last half mile. For the first time she thinks of the angel, the angel of justice with the flaming sword who guards the gate. She wonders if the angel will have disappeared, leaving the gate unguarded and the long vista across the garden open to her eager gaze. Or maybe the angel will be waiting to welcome her; waiting to bow and greet her solemnly as angels do, or did.

Now she sees the long curve of the garden wall and the exquisite bridge where the eastward river leaves the garden. At the centre of the garden is a fountain, and from the fountain flow the four rivers that divide the garden into quarters, and flow out under the wall. She walks around in the deep shade of the wall towards the gate and the angel.

The angel is leaning against the gatepost, relaxed, wings furled back. The angel seems relaxed, not so much on guard as waiting. The angel's sword has been thrust into the ground, point down. The blade glows hot-copper-coloured like the angel's hair. There is a dark awe in angels; a solemnity, a magnificence. The angel knew what she had done: knew she had grinned complicitly at the serpent; knew she had eaten the apple, its juices pouring down her chin; knew she had eaten it laughing, greedy as a child. God might understand, but the angel would be simply appalled. God might forgive but the angel, stern and competent, would only obey. The angel was pure as neither God nor Eve would ever be, less inclined to apples and sex and laughter . . . Encounters with angels are strange and hard to understand. Suddenly Eve wants none of it.

This is her home. She is free to return. But still she feels both shy and proud. The angel had driven her out and mounted guard over her home. She had been expelled and the angel had been made protector of the garden. Eve does not want to talk to the angel, nor to be shown round by the angel. She wants to slip in on her own and take possession. She backs away from the gate, slips closer to the wall, retreats around the long curve until the angel is out of sight. She walks to the next bridge. Then she climbs the wall. She knows this would not be possible if it were not permissible. She is not breaking in like a thief in the night, she is coming privately, quietly.

So, now, she is sitting on the wall and looking down into her garden. Her feet are dangling into Eden, her toes twisting with pleasure. It is lovelier than she had let herself remember. It is waiting for her. It has form and symmetry, so subtle that it seems entirely unplanned, random like the rest of the universe. She looks around with perfect attention, then smiles. Through a stand of trees, she catches sight of the giant nest they had built themselves to play in, woven into the sturdy branches of an ilex tree. She remembers sharply the first time they had made love, rocked gently within it. Tears spring to her eyes, an easy nostalgic happiness.

In the middle of the garden, up the green ride, the fountain rises, pluming high and falling back into its great green bowl, then pouring out of the lips of the bowl and forming the four rivers. Close beside the fountain the Tree still grows. She had leaned back against the marble bowl and laughed when the serpent first spoke to her.

The tree of the knowledge of good and evil.

In the twilight the fruit of the tree glows gently, inviting, beguiling. It is too far away for her to catch the intoxicating scent of it, but she knows, knows exactly how it will smell. Her mouth fills with saliva, warm and wet, and the longing is on her; but she also knows that this time she will not eat of that tree, because she has learned a lot including self-discipline and how to measure consequence against cause and draw cold conclusions. It is probably better so.

She prepares to jump down from the wall into the garden. She looks between her own knees to the soft grass below, judging the distance. She pauses, poised. Suddenly her focus shifts from the waiting grass to her own ankle; to the inside of her ankle; to just above the bump of bone. There is a tangled knot of veins there, bruised plum colour. From the ugly knot a single blue vein runs upwards towards her knee. Her eye follows it. Her knees are lumpy, and she has a triangular scar just above the kneecap. She recalls the frightening wedge of skin that had flapped away from the deep painful cut and how she had held it down, pushing it back into place with her wrist, while Adam ran up the hill, panic in his eyes while he shouted not to panic. Further up she cannot see her pubic hair because her stomach folds outwards hiding it, but she can see how her breasts pull down and the skin beside her armpits is pale from their weight. She looks at the back of her hands as they lie tidily at the ends of her arms, resting on the moss of the wall. Her fingernails have yellowed, broken and chipped, the pearly cuticles have nearly disappeared; but they are strong hands, her hands, toughened through work.

She will jump, she thinks, she will jump now, down into her garden; she will jump back into paradise and her veins will vanish; the scar will disappear. Her stomach will flatten and firm, her breasts will shrink and rise. She will jump into the garden that was made for her, and forget the orchard she made for herself. She will be a child again, innocent and lovely and sexy. She will have no past. No desire. No pain. Nothing will ever happen, except they might build a new tree house.

She thinks about it, glowing.

Then without even knowing she has made a decision, she finds she has turned round, scrambled off the wall on the outside of the garden and is walking away. She knows why, too. She is not happy but she is very certain. She cannot desert the woman she has become; the body she inhabits, the struggles, the losses, and the little gains, the life, she has created for herself. She does not want to. If nothing ever happens it will be very dull. Some days she will come and sit on the wall again like that and pretend, but she chooses not to return.

She never tells Adam about it. It is her first secret. She does not tell him that the bleeding has stopped, that the curse is lifted, and that he does not rule her any more. That was not his business. She knew him, he would want to go back. He liked perfection. Not her. She would rather be a grandmother. Going forward was more interesting than being happy.

Years ago she had eaten the apple. No one really understood: she ate the apple because she was curious, because she wanted to know what would happen if she did, what would happen next. She ate the apple because the snake's slitty-eyed smile was not simple, not pure.

Knowledge is never there in your hand, never complete and waiting to be eaten: knowledge is like a garden, always growing, changing, in-the-making. And still, despite everything, still . . . she wants to know what will happen next.

Loving Oedipus

OF COURSE I KNEW.

They say a mother always knows.

From the first moment, when – standing in the sunlit courtyard – I saw the running messenger, his hair shaven as the bearer of ill tidings, but something in his pace alive and joyful. I knew then.

I had time to withdraw before the messenger topped the steep roadway up the acropolis and puffed into the atrium. I heard him gasp out, panting, that he must speak with the Lady Jocasta.

A limping stranger had killed the King, my husband. A heroic stranger had outwitted the Sphinx, who had cast herself wailing into the sea and would afflict the people no longer. Given that the King had been doddery and ineffective and that the Sphinx had been neither, but dangerous and merciless instead, it is not surprising that the joy of one delivery had wiped out the grief of the other.

'Will you marry him, Lady?' asked my maids as they brushed my hair that evening. 'We have seen him.'

'What is he like?' I made myself sound languid.

'He's young,' said the younger of the two, 'he's very young and he's a cripple; there's something wrong with his feet.'

'He's very young,' said the other, and she smiled a slow sly smile, so I knew he was sexy.

'Will you marry him?' they asked.

'Oh yes,' I said. Then, lest I had sounded suspiciously eager, I added, 'I'll have to; the patricians will make me.' They would of course, which was convenient. 'I think,' I said, 'that you should re-shape my eyebrows.' The second maid smiled knowingly, and reached for perfumed oil and face creams.

Three days of mourning. They re-shaped my eyebrows, vanished my greying hairs, looked out my jewels. I, I waited.

He limped across the pavement; the fountain sang sweet in the sunlight, casting fragments of radiance across the flags. He bowed and looked at me. I smiled. I caught deep in his eyes an answering smile. My child come home. My son. My beloved. Both, and I was wild with the forbidden desire.

'Lady,' he said. He did not know, though his eyebrows too rose thick like flicked wings towards his forehead. But mine had been carefully plucked straight.

I knew. He did not know.

'What do they call you?' I inquired.

'The Stranger,' he said, and then laughed. 'No, it's an ugly name really. They call me Oedipus, Puffy Feet.'

Tenderness was always at the root of my desire for him. Tenderness and guilt – a powerful aphrodisiac. A bottomless guilt and an overwhelming tenderness; they caught at my stomach, churning it as it had not been churned since before he was born. I wanted to touch his feet, to cradle them in my hands, stroke them, run my fingers over the deep scars where his father had hammered in the bolt and hanged him, head down, from the ilex tree. I wanted to take away the furrows of habitual pain that ran from the inner edge of his nostrils to the outer corners of his mouth. I had chiselled those lines myself, when I let my first husband snatch him, right from between my thighs, his head still damp, cord still trailing, his legs rucked up like a rabbit's, but each toe tiny and round like pink peas in a pod. I wanted him inside me again.

'I am perhaps a little old for you,' I said, still smiling. 'Don't let the patricians force your hand. You could run away tonight.'

'No,' he said. 'I could, but I won't. I want this Kingdom,' he said. It was true: he was ambitious, greedy and – although he did not know it – home at last. He grinned widely and I knew he also wanted this Kingdom because I was the Queen.

I wanted him too – ah, yes – so we were married.

He was good at being the King. It does not matter if the King is lame. It does matter for the Hero, but he did not need to be the Hero, because he was the Saviour and so could be wise and just instead. He alone of all men had answered the Sphinx's silly riddle and that seemed a good proof of intelligence, far more useful to the people than if he had wanted to lead them off into the extravagant and pointless wars that Heroes tend to need even after they become Kings. So the people loved him; fatherless, he was a careful father and he loved them.

Lameness matters for the Suitor too, but not the Husband. His wife loved him and he loved her. We were very happy.

I held him against my breast and murmured those things that a woman murmurs to her child and to her lover. I touched him and stroked and fondled him in all the places and in all the ways that I had not been able to do when he was baby, watching and doting.

Once half-embarrassed by his own delight and my coddling, my petting, my teasing fingers, he looked sheepish and said, 'I'm afraid that sexually half of me is still a little boy.'

I smiled, held him and teased, 'That's why we suit. I'm afraid that sexually half of me is a bossy mummy.'

Only half. Only half, for each of us. There was harsh passion too. I was open for him. Broken open, and yet wanting to be more open.

'Deeper,' I would growl to him, rutting. 'Deeper. Come on in, come in further, harder, deeper.'

He would laugh, 'I'm not Priapus,' he would say, glancing at the secret shrine we kept in the privacy of our chamber.

'You are for me.' I'd pull him on to me, into me.

'I'll hurt you.'

'Women can get babies through there. I'm not afraid of you.'

'You should be,' he'd say, pushing in deeper, further, harder.

But I never was. I liked to feel him in there, pushing, pushing against my cervix as he had pushed the other way, pushing in and in where he had once pushed out. I wanted him deeper inside me, and further, and again and again, and my deepest muscles quivered, danced and contracted for him again as then. They held him now with all the power that they had pushed him with before, and my body sang and buzzed and softened for the joy of him.

Tenderness, I said before: and yes, there was at the heart of our loving, at the core of our sex, a deep tenderness which carried us through his pain and my ageing; through the wounds of his lonely childhood and the scars of my loveless marriage. A hot and tender love. We came to each other bitter and we made each other sweet.

We talked, entwined, close, his hard angles against my soft curves – they fit well together, young men and older women.

'I killed your husband,' he'd say, 'I'm sorry I killed your husband.'

'I'm not,' I'd answer, stroking his dark head.

'I didn't mean to kill him, you know. He was . . . he was in his chariot, so high and mighty; he was driving down on me, he shouted to me to clear out of his way as though I were a child, a cheeky little brat and he was my father. He had no right to speak to me like that, but I should not have killed him. His arrogance made me mad. I'm bad like that – when I was a child I was always getting in fights because I could not bear anyone to laugh at me.'

'I won't laugh at you,' I'd promise, and he'd suck at my

breasts to comfort the child in him, to encourage the telling, as a child needs to.

'Because . . . partly because they used to say I was not a real prince, just adopted from nowhere, taken in from nothing.' I would weep silently for what I had done to my baby. I had failed to protect him from his father.

'And partly . . .' a long pause now in the dark. I hold my breath, cradle his head against my nipple. I listen in the silence to the shame of the crippled which is the hardest thing they have to bear; the shame which we whose legs and feet and arms are lovely lay on them, the burden of our good luck which shames us and we make them carry our shame '. . . and partly because of my, because of my . . . my feet.' He had earlier in the night proved he is a man, but now he is all child again, open and exposed again. I would be shaken with guilt and grief. I had inflicted those wounds – the wounds in his feet and the wounds in his heart. My fault. And I would hold the sad little boy against my bosom and the lovely young man in my arms and I would kiss it all better, there on his round baby cheeks and there on his full sexy mouth and I would get joy from both the kissings and he would be comforted.

'I've always had a foul temper.' But now he'd be grinning in the dark, ashamed, proud and relieved to have confessed both. 'But I should not have killed him.'

I want to say like a mother, 'It was very naughty, but I love you. You must learn to keep your temper, but I still love you.'

I want to say like a lover, 'I'm glad you killed him. I love you.'

I want to say like a mother and a lover together, I want to say like a wife, who is all too often both mother and lover, 'There, there,' and 'It's all right now.'

Sometimes, though, it was me who was guilty in the night. I'd wake up screaming and he would be there, holding me like a child, murmuring, stroking, saying, 'What is it? What is it?'

Sleepy, frightened, crying, my guard down, I would tell him, 'You are my baby and I let them take you away. I let them nail your feet and hang you from a tree. I let them take you away and I will never see you again.' And he would half-smile and hug me close and say, 'But you can see me again. I'm here. I'm here to stay. It's just a dream, a nasty dream. There, there. It's all right now.'

I really did not expect to get pregnant. I thought I would be too old. The first time I was frightened. They tell horrible stories about babies like ours. Blind or with two heads or with no brains. Or even worse – little monsters, like children of the Sphinx. However much you love them they cannot be allowed to live. And, too, a child like that would make people curious; they would wonder, they would . . . I was frightened and the nightmares were worse, and Oedipus was worried, anxious for me.

But she was born, our first child, Antigone. She was perfect; tiny and perfect and I held her with exhausted delight and then Oedipus came, came limping towards the bed, and I was tired and confused and still far away in that place where women have to go to get their children, and he rose up beside the bed and reached for my baby and I thought he was his own father and would snatch her away, again, and I was screaming and he was hurt, baffled, alarmed, and they had to hold me down and I fainted. But when I opened my eyes, he was holding her, holding her and laughing with delight. Her father and her big brother both at once and I knew that I was safe and he would love her with tenderness and she would love him and never leave him and I might even perhaps have been jealous, but I was not. Now he could laugh at me and reassure himself; it was just childbirth, just pain and he understood all about that, so he laughed at me and forgave me, because I had given him his daughter. It makes it a little easier to know that when I am gone Antigone will take care of him, will not leave him, whatever happens and he will love her, uncontaminated. They both have an openness, a faithfulness, that I cannot rise to.

We had four children, and he was still as lovely and young and good as the day he limped back into my life, and I loved him. It was a good time for a time. Then, one spring, the lambs in the hill pastures were born deformed. I saw some – it was horrible. There were odd whispers of unease. That summer it stayed dank and cold far too long and the crops failed, and the fruit trees did not set. There was a dark rust on the grapes and they did not sweeten. The ancient olive trees dropped their silver leaves too early and looked hungry and spiked. The sound of the whispers swelled. The unease settled on the people, and when the fever came too many just turned their faces to the wall and died.

'Leave it,' I said to his restless inquiries. 'It's just one bad year.' But he could not leave it because he was a good king, and because the next year was worse.

Oedipus sent for Tiresias, the prophet-priest; the blind woman-man who knew everything – past, present and future. He had been old when my first husband had consulted with him, learned that his own son would kill him, and stolen my baby from me. I remembered him stern and aweful, but now he was so old that he was kind, gentle, even then, even knowing. Sad, he sounded, sad and tender when he told Oedipus that he had killed his father and married his mother so that there was a curse on all the Kingdom that could not be lifted by charm or sacrifice or spell or journey or offering or repentance or death. A curse that could not be lifted.

Oedipus stood motionless while Tiresias told him, and stayed so afterwards when the old prophet fell silent. Then he turned and looked for me; for his mother and his beloved. I moved toward him, but when I touched him I knew his horror. He looked at me, cool and clear, waiting, attentive. He knew me too well; when he looked he saw, and seeing he knew that I had always known.

He growled, like an animal, he said, 'You knew.' And he hit me, twice, across the face, hard swinging blows. They hurt. I stumbled, fell. He did not move from the spot. He bent forward, vomited and started to howl like a dog; then with his own hands he . . . I thought he was covering his face, but he . . . his hands were foul with his own sick and he . . . he tore his eyes out with his own fingers and rushed out into the night.

Perhaps I should have told him first, but I could not. I do not think it would have made any difference. The last thing he saw was me and he was disgusted. He looked at me and it was a look of total loathing: not even hatred, just disgust. Because of that look, I will hang myself tonight, and travel into the land of the dead alone.

Tiresias took my hand in his, a gentle ancient dryness. He said, 'You knew.'

'Yes.'

'It was wrong.'

'Yes.'

'Then why?'

'I wanted him. I needed him. Is it wrong to take what you need?'

'Sometimes.' There was a pause. I felt his love and his condemnation. 'It will be better if the people believe you did not know. I will never tell anyone,' he promised.

Then he half-smiled and said, 'So it is true, what they say, that a mother always knows. I have never been a mother; it is something I don't know about.' He was asking, so at last I was honest.

'No,' I said, 'that isn't how I knew. I knew because you told us. I believe in prophecy. Two lifetimes ago you told my first husband that his son would kill him. As soon as I saw the messenger's shaved head; even before he said, "A limping stranger has killed the King," I knew. I had been waiting. Mothers don't always know. Lovers don't ever know. I had only one god and it was him, and he did not know. But prophets know, the gods speak through them and they speak truly. You can trust the prophets.'

'Yes,' said Tiresias.

He took his rope from around his waist and handed it to me and we both wept.

Having Sex with a Saint

~

I TOOK A WOMAN HOME the other night. This surprised me – it is not the sort of thing I do any more. I feel I am too old: past the age for romantic or sexual adventures. After Ella left I gave up I suppose; or at least I stopped investing in it; stopped looking, expecting or even hoping. On the whole I find friendship more than adequate; real old friendships with deep roots and sweet fruit – friendship leads to excellent dinner parties, affectionate but authentic conversation, a little too much drink, no drama and getting home before the pumpkin-hour.

But I took a woman home the other night. We met at a party: the sort of party that is vaguely work-related, where you know slightly less than half the far too many people; and you talk too loud and drink too much and wonder why you came. I wasn't out on the pull (I love this vulgar phrase) or anything. I'm not sure how we got talking; I'm not sure at what point I thought she was coming on to me; I'm not sure how it happened. She seemed so open, so eager, so generous. As though she was giving herself away. Free. I did feel flattered, but even more I felt tender; she seemed so transparent, I want to say 'innocent' but that is the wrong word . . . so are 'fragile', 'delicate' and 'vulnerable'. Something about her anyway made me think sharply about sex and what fun it could be, and at the same time I felt warmly rather than hotly towards her. So we left the party together. As we were leaving my friend Kathy gave me a hug and whispered, 'Be careful, Jenny' in my ear. It was too noisy to pursue it. I sensed it as general congratulation rather than warning. I grinned and felt gleeful and clever. Then I took her home.

She had no breasts. 'Cancer?' I asked tentatively as I made her coffee and poured myself a whisky. No, not cancer, she had had them cut off, and her womb removed too, her vagina sewn up. Sexless so that she could be all the sexes. She said. I froze for a moment, looking at my very charming French provincial tiles above the sink. I thought what in heaven's name had I got myself in to. Then I took a slug of the whisky, and suddenly instead of feeling alarmed I felt a pure curiosity that was itself tantamount to an erotic charge. I put down both coffee and whisky and then kissed her; her lips were slightly salty, her teeth felt small and tidy. She was voluptuously passive. It was a fabulous kiss; I could feel her wanting it, absorbing it, pulling me out of myself and towards her, in to her. It had, I thought, been a long time, too long a time.

It was all in slow motion – no greed, no rush. Later, on the sofa, I undid the buttons of her blouse, one by one, carefully. The heavy linen hung straight down; even with the buttons undone the two sides did not fall apart. I had to separate them like a curtain. She was very slender; her skin seemed to cover her minimally, stretched, undulating slightly over her ribs. It was like alabaster, translucent, creamy, very pale. Her collar bone stood out, so that there were blue shadows beneath it; and deep in one of the shadows was a dark mole. I touched it gently. Her eyes looked huge and moist. She kept them fixed on mine; daring me, but tenderly, to look at her, to look at her, to drown in the delight of my own gaze.

She had no breasts, no nipples and barely any scarring. She had a zip. It ran from where her left nipple should have been, down across her alabaster skin at a slight slant, so that it crossed her waistline where her navel should have been and ended about where my appendix scar is. It looked like a perfectly ordinary, medium-weight zip – neat little silvery interlocking metal teeth. It had been beautifully inserted – no puckering, no visible stitches. At the top end, flat on her ribs, was the metal loop with a small black leather tag to make undoing it easier.

She smiled, lay down on the carpet, tidily her arms stretched straight out on either side, her legs straight and feet crossed at the ankles.

'Unzip me,' she said, 'please.'

I hesitated, enchanted, a little scared, driven by nerves and desire. I reached out, took the leather tag and very slowly pulled it down.

She was open to me, completely open. I could peel back her skin, lift out her ribs one by one, laying them in a neat pile beside us. She breathed slowly, calmly, trustingly. Warm, her innards were warm, pulsing, steaming slightly though my room was not cold. I buried my hands to the wrist in yards of soft intestine; they felt silky and alive. I could feel the rhythm of her life against my relaxed knuckles, a firm irregular vibration against my finger tips, pulsing.

'One day,' I said, 'someone won't put it all back. You'll die. You should be more careful.' I was tempted to rip it all out, chuck her insides around the room, ruin her. 'You should be more careful,' I said it with a kind of agony – envy and fear together.

She laughed, 'I hope so,' she said, 'ah, strewn, tossed to the wind, everyone's everywhere. Go on. Please.'

But I lost the impulse. Lost my nerve. It was so warm and soft. Like a child I went exploring. Her arms stayed straight out, but I could tell her pleasure in the tiny twitches and responses of the long muscles, and the wave motion of her oesophagus as she swallowed. I held her heart in my hand and she smiled. There were no boundaries and no barriers. I held her heart in my hand and it nearly broke my heart. Hers lay pumping there, firmer than I had expected, a tough muscle doing its work – beating steadily. The veins and arteries ran between my fingers trailing down back into her body. Her heart thumped against my palm. She was open, open and not broken and she gave herself to me, with total abandonment. She abandoned herself and gave herself to me with absolute trust or absolute despair and they were perhaps, nearly, maybe, almost, the same thing.

Did I feel cruel? Did I feel a temptation to, a weighting towards, cruelty? I would come to feel cruel I think, if I saw her much, too often. There was something in that self-giving that would provoke one: that would make one want to push it, push her, to a point where she would say stop, where she would have to acknowledge that no one, no one could go all the way, could be that generous, that it was too dangerous, that there were limits, boundaries, barriers. But no, actually at the time I did not feel cruel. I felt that tenderness that I feel for very small babies when they are asleep, because I know that with a little pressure, with one thumb I could crush in their skulls, smash through the fontanel, kill them. And the power makes me kindly, makes we weep for their danger. But at the same time, this is one reason why I never had babies myself. I do not know how far I could trust myself.

Almost regretfully I put everything back, like a child's jigsaw puzzle. 'Not there,' she said once, 'that's my spleen – up there, further up, it goes up there.' It did; I needed both hands and had to push her lung aside; I could hear the sigh as her breath was pressed out. When I released the pressure I could feel the lung inflating again, inspired, pushing my hand up, and when I stiffened my wrist, exerted a counter-pressure, the blue-red mass deflated, retreated and the thin sound of the air flowed over her tongue. I was breathing her and she was entirely relaxed, accepting, passive. I reached for a rib from the pile and tried to work out how to slot it in, click it down against her spine. I looked at her inquiringly; but her eyes were glazed, and I had to work it out for myself.

I pulled the zip up very slowly. She gave a tiny sigh and a long shiver. She was having an orgasm. Did she I wondered have a clitoris? I looked at the neat sewn line between her legs that closed off her vagina, and could not guess. 'No,' she said with her eyes still shut, 'it's everywhere – everywhere.' Then she uncrossed her ankles, stood up gracefully, put her clothes on neatly and left.

I was so angry. Angry, raging, livid – a fury, a demon. I was Lilith in my wrath, a vampire bat, a wolf, a lethal venom, a bird of prey, talons sharpened. She should not dare – no one should dare. The risk, her risk, put me at risk. Put my ego at risk. Put ego itself at risk. Me, I want to be inviolate, violet and pale mauves, cabined in the real, cribbed within my own flesh, confined to the due limits of the self. Not scarlet and purple; not open, broken, strewn across the desert. Inside there is me – inside my skin, my boundary – and outside there is Other, the forest, the storm. I wear my skin like an armour and armadillo my way through the world, though sights and sounds and smells and tastes pour in and snot and words and shit and blood pour out through orifices I do not dare to seal. They are border frontiers. You need a visa to come in. I need a passport to go out. No illegal immigrants within my borders – boarders, pirates, smugglers, asylum seekers. I police the borders with hygiene, with distance, coldness and morality.

But she . . . I am shaken. Shaken by her generosity, foolhardy dangerous generosity; by her refusal to withhold her gifts, by her liminality, her strangeness. I am shaken, angry and defeated.

In the morning I found a small piece. It had got hidden under a sofa cushion. I must have been more excited than I'd realised – I thought I had been so careful. I don't know what it was, something a bit nubbly, cold now, sort of clotted. I wrapped it in a skin of cling film and kept it in the fridge for a while. I thought she might come back for it. But no, she just gave herself away, in both senses of that phrase. After a while it dried out, shrivelled, desiccated; it looked like old dog poo – hard, dark-coloured. And in the end I threw it out.

I never saw her again.

Maid Marion's Story

'MOTHER,' says the newest novice shyly. 'Mother, is it true . . .' she hesitates. She is a lovely child, still leggy and slightly clumsy like a colt, brightly innocent. There are light freckles across her nose. Her hair is touched with the red bronze of autumn beech masts and she has the longest fattest plait that I have seen since I cut my own off and ran away to the Greenwood, hardly older than she is now.

I get on very well with the novices. It is harder with the older women. You can't spend more than half your life shinning up trees, shooting your supper with a longbow and singing in the Greenwood and then expect other women to feel easy. Not if they are women who, while you were living so, were veiled, confined, restricted, their white hands fluttering over their stitchcraft. I went from a motherless house to a boys' realm and never learned the ways of women: my sisters know this, it makes them both envious and appalled. But the little girls, the novices, the girls the age my daughters would be if only I had had any, I get on well with them.

'Mother,' says the newest novice, more boldly now, 'is it true? Is it true that you lived in the Greenwood with

Robin of Locksley and the Merrie Men?' She glows, excited, star-struck, 'With the *real* Robin Hood?' She gasps.

'Yes,' I say. 'Yes,' in as neutral a voice as I can manage. It is no secret, but I do not want these silly children to get carried away.

It is too late. 'My hero,' sighs the newest novice, her eyes wide and bright. How Robin would like this.

'My husband,' I say firmly, trying to make it sound dull.

'But not when you were in the forest, Mother.' The voice sounds polite enough – but there is something else. I look up sharply. It is an older novice, a pretty, fair, pink face, but with little close-watching eyes. When they catch mine she gives me a wink, so sly, so . . . so lewd that I have to breathe in, through my nose as quick and quiet as I can, before I say, apparently unruffled:

'No, Edith, not then.' I said to her, 'That's well known. He swore an oath to my father, and we had to wait until King Richard came home.' But she knows, that one, that she has caught me out somehow, though I doubt she knows quite how. What she knows she will use.

All this flows over the sweet head of the sweet little novice. She is still saying 'ooh' and 'ah' and 'Oh, Mother,' with her eyes all shining. Why have her family sent her here so young, so half-formed and so vital? Why have we accepted her? 'Oh mother,' she says, 'how lovely. Oh lucky you.'

And I tap her affectionately on the nose with my ringed

finger and I say, a little teasingly, 'I bet you think it was always May in Sherwood Forest.'

'Mother,' she says reprovingly, almost hurt in her disappointment, 'you sound like my mother.'

I foolishly soften, melt, drift a little, and stroke her head and – perhaps for me as much as for her – say:

'Child, you need to see it whole. If it is true, and I believe it is true still, that there is no lovelier thing in all the world than the sun on the soft beech leaves at dawn in Sherwood in May; then it is also true that there is nothing as disagreeable as that same beechwood on a rainy November evening when the damp is in your spine, and the supper has not been shot yet and the men you live among decide to play yet another childish and very dangerous game.'

I hear the edge in my own voice, sense the tension in the girls, but luckily the bell rings for Vespers. The novices' recreation hour is over and we go, decorous and ladylike, to chapel.

But they have disturbed me, the novices. I am not sure if it was the starry-eyed excitement of the little one, or the narrow-eyed prurience of Mademoiselle Edith; but through Vespers and supper I am fretful, filled with a restlessness that neither a complicated session with the account books nor the candle-lit simplicity of Compline can soothe.

After the Great Silence – the long hush of the monastic night – has settled on the priory, I wrap myself in a cloak and go out, gliding through the door and over the wall as I used to do once from my father's house. Now, as then, I slip off to find Robin in the forest.

It is a huge indigo blue night. The moon is not yet up; the sky is clear and starry. There is no wind, but a softness in the air. Within the enclosure walls it is silent, but outside there is a rustling and a fussing in the undergrowth. There is never true silence in a living wood . . . perhaps it is the sound of trees themselves growing and dying, that low throb or soft dark hum. Something moves in the Greenwood, something dark but beautiful. Even now I am old and respectable and sleep in a high bed and the wind cannot reach through the curtains, the forest still calls to me. It says, 'Come out, come in, come back.'

Although it is dark I find Robin's grave, the low green mound that Little John dug in the green grass for him. Around the grave, blurred by the night, there are little bunches of wild flowers. I think that a fallen oak branch has been blown against the mound, but as I reach to pull it clear I realise it is an antler from a noble stag. Point downwards, plunged into the ground at his feet are half-a-dozen good arrows; a waste I think, but the young men around here believe it will bring them luck – in hunting or in war – to offer Robin's ghost a fresh-feathered arrow from each new quiverful.

When we first buried him I had a fine stone cut: 'Here lies Robert, Earl of Huntingdon and Lord of the Manor of Locksley. Jesu mercy, Mary pray.' But night after night it was defaced. In the end I ordered a new one. Now it says 'Robin Hood': nothing else. No one has so much as scratched it since: even in death he is not mine, but theirs, everyone's.

I never kneel here. I sit on the ground with my legs crossed like a little girl, not praying but thinking and remembering.

I remember Edith's knowing wink. I blush, not as she would think, as most people would think and as I would not blame them for thinking. I blush not because she has hit home, but because she is so wide of the mark. I was never Robin's lover and that was no choice of mine.

I remember the newest novice and see my own index finger tap her freckled nose. I smile now a little ruefully for though what I said was true and needed saying, in truth, for me as for her, it is always May in Sherwood Forest.

The musky sharp scent of the wild garlic, with white flowers like stars in the green dark shadows under the waterfall. Through the slim blanched trunks of birch trees, in the distance great sweeps of bluebells like fallen skies. Out in the open clearings the snake-headed fritillaries like butterflies among the cowslips. Scuttle of squirrel; ear twitch of passing doe; three thrush fledglings lined up by their parents on spray of flowering gean to see the sunshine and to learn to sing.

In May in Sherwood Forest I wake early and walk out through the Greenwood; silent through the pines, rustling through the winter-dried fall of oak leaves. I look up through the lace and filigree of beech twigs and new beech leaves and the bright sun makes the green leaves greener; and that freshest of all fresh greens deepens the blue of the sky. In May in Sherwood Forest I sit me down in the bright morning, cradled between the cool, smooth grey roots of the beech trees, soft in the jewel green moss, and it is Eden again and I wish that Robin would come to me eager and unashamed.

He comes. He comes like a child, with all his friends, laughing, singing, boisterous and smiling; and suddenly the tender moment is gone and we are up and doing – an adventure, a competition, a game, a hunt, a picnic. He never grew up; never wanted to come in from the Forest. He could never settle down, even afterwards when I thought we would come back to Locksley and make up for lost time; babies, a dairy with fat cows, a big loom, a proper harp. I thought he wanted to be a husband and to be at peace. But he was bored and restless and looking for trouble. If you look for trouble you find it.

Sometimes I think that I had to make my choices too young; and with no mother to guide me. I grew up knowing Robin. He was my brother, neighbour, friend, teacher, hero and sweetheart. At sixteen I did not have any way of knowing that all that does not necessarily add up to lover or to husband.

So there I was, with my wedding wreath in my hair and a seemly hush in the Chapel. Suddenly there are soldiers and sheriffs and green-clad strangers. A fat clerk is reading a vellum document which denounces my boyfriend as outlaw, poacher and traitor. My father is shouting. Guy is laughing in his moustaches and looking both smug and lecherous, which is scary when you are sixteen.

And in all the hubbub, in front of all these people, strangers and my closest family together, Robin turns to me and says, 'Choose.' Now. And shy, ignorant, romantic, desperately wanting to do the right thing, and with his shining eyes upon me, I chose.

And then, with no one asking me, I hear Robin making his preposterous oath, the stupid unnecessarily noble promise, that he will take me as a wife from no hand but the King's; and will keep me as a chaste child until then. Perhaps he could not have known that 'until then' would be nearly twenty years. More likely he would not have cared. And Robin could never have been forsworn.

My father was a noisy braggart. He could scarcely have made it worse for himself. With his shouting and threatening and bluster, he pushed me over a line. By then I had had him wound round my little finger for years. But I have wished sometimes that he had done as he threatened – locked me up and married me to Guy. Then Robin could have been a tragic true lover, a role that would have suited him, and I could have had a life.

I have learned to understand. Robin wrote the story, he gave us our parts and we played them. He was a true legend, a real hero. And what did it lead to? To Will Scarlet dead for loyalty; Guy dead for villainy: Little John half-mad and banished to Ireland for friendship. My dear Friar really did always want to be a hermit by the river, not a fat libertine in a farce. Even Robin couldn't do much about the kings – neither John nor Richard – though he tried. History keeps tabs on kings; you cannot really turn them into bit parts in your own legend. But my goodness Robin gave it a good shot. And I, I was the love interest, the romantic moment, and I played my part and stayed slim and true and golden and pure; so now I am immured in a nunnery, childless and cross, for romance.

In the cool of the night I feel old and bitter. My knees ache as I stand up and pull my cloak around me. Then something happens.

The moon rises, abruptly over the dense crown of the ancient oak trees. The nunnery buildings are splashed in pale light, the upper line of windows sharply black; and I realise that Robin could not have shot an arrow from that window and had it land here. It is simply not possible. Arrows always fly in straight lines.

I remember the scene with vivid clarity. Robin bleeding in John's arms; the silver horn rolling silent on the floor. John weeping. Me weeping. And Robin bending the great yew bow for the last time. 'Where the arrow falls, there bury me,' he whispers, shoots and dies. And I, who knew him so very, very well, even I felt no surprise when John showed me the arrow well beyond the enclosure wall, standing in the most perfect place, in a little green clearing under the Greenwood tree, a thrush's nest overhead and acorns scattered at his feet. The very place where the noble hero ought to lie.

Now I am not old and bitter, and it is not a chilly night. I am young and golden and it is always May in the Greenwood. There is no lovelier thing in all the world than Sherwood Forest in the May time and I could have no better story.

I am laughing and laughing. Now I know absolutely and with certainty that the newest novice is right and Edith's slime won't stick. I am and I will be forever Maid Marion, Robin's Queen in the Greenwood. I go back to my cell a happy, laughing woman.

Robin was a genius.

Don't believe everything you hear about Guy of Gisbourne either. He was a very sexy man.

Sybil

DELPHI AT DAWN. Dark blue morning. Day still hidden. Still cool, but heat waiting.

Blue. Brown. Gold. Black. White. Hard colours. Clear. Bright.

This is the navel of the world. The omphalos.

Here the twin eagles met, released by Zeus from the dawn horizon. And from the place of sunset beyond the farthest shores. They flew towards each other, wing beat matched to wing beat, unerring and identical, from the courts of morning and the stables of the sun. They met at Delphi. The centre of the world, the epicentre, the silent space in the whirling storm of history. The navel. Here the life of the outside, the bright day of politics and wars and kingdoms and marriages and narratives is joined to the dark beginnings, the womb of the life and the dreams and the madness of the gods. The omphalos.

Ah, come on! We all know what the 'navel' is a euphemism for. The stone omphalos is set up in the centre of the Temple of Apollo, a rough pillar like a finger or a prick. It is adorned with oil and flowers. But nearby is the deep crack, the fissure in the solid ground, the steaming slit, and from its depths the voice of the god speaks to men through a woman. A naked woman who crouches over the pit. A woman who is also a snake, the pythia. A woman whom the gods possess and who speaks not her own words but theirs. A woman ecstatic, crazed, raving, and who needs the well-oiled palms of the priests to deliver the word – cleaned, washed, tidied, clothed in rhythm and sense, alive and useful to the anxiously watching city fathers.

Be clear. Delphi is the holy place. Below on the plain the olive groves ring, sing, a sea of grey; and out beyond the enclosed places, out there shining, dancing, flat, the bay – the sea of blue.

This is the holy place. This is the place where the god speaks, audible if not comprehensible; this is the place that the cities have not wrested from the wild; this is the place that the fathers have not stolen from the mothers; this is the place where the categories have collapsed and language with them, and sense and rhythm and reason and culture, and where, out of chaos, not order but fierce beauty comes and none can name it, or hold it, or apprehend it.

This is the holy place, the holiest place of all. And so it is a venal, cynical, avaricious greedy place too; for wherever gods and mortals meet the lives and shapes of history and eternity are bent, warped, twisted out of true. Wherever there's a crack in the seamless membrane between time and eternity, whenever that membrane is split or punctured, power flows through, both ways, and chaos follows, and the two languages which cannot be emulsified entangle, knot, skein, embrace – clumsy, exuberant, monstrous, mean – and they spark, crash and toss out explosions of purity, holiness, silence, awe, but-and-also the purity of the dark – lust, death, lies, deceit, conceit and everywhere power, power and power.

This is the holy place. In the piggy eyes of its priests, and the corrupt desires of its devotees and in the shameless mockery of us fifty-year-old *kore* and in the ambiguities and shuffling of the god himself and in the bribes and politics and spies and cheats, the holiness of the place and its everlasting silences are fulfilled. Not nice. Not how we would like it. But there it is. Don't go looking for the straight when you walk the inturned coils of the sacred and stand before the three-legged tripod. Don't look for the straightforward when you look into the eyes of a god.

I know. I am Pythia, the snake priestess of the shrine of Delphi and I know everything and I know nothing and I know they are the same thing. I know all this because I am mad and because I know I am mad which is the first proof that I am not mad.

my periods ceased.

and suddenly i snapped – poing! tsk! crack! – i snapped the restrictions of my story.

the waning moon pulls; the sand sucks and sings on the beach. the waves pull tug yearn for the moon, for the pure passivity. for the sea of tranquillity to fill and fill and be emptied. to pause, pure, purified, bloodless. to lean long and lean into the oceans to be weighted into the rhythm of what was and is and now as surprising as the origin will not be again.

the moon, the moon waxes, wanes, wails, specific but unstable. But not me i've snapped the cord, cut the bond, the cord that bound me, the cord that corded me, cored me to mother, a mother, the mother, another, mother, moth, mother, mummy, mamma, mmm and mmm-mmm, but no. no i'm free.

let the bitch pack, the wolf girls, howl and howl to the shadowed perfection of the full moon. let the lovers claw, grope, scratch to the finer nail the paring, pairing moon. not me. i'm free.

free now. fifty years . . . half a century or centuries . . . i've been a woman – *kore, parthenos, gune, meter* – bound to the rhythm, to the beat, to the drum. not now. i'm free – free to, free from, free for, free fall.

well who would love a fickle mistress? me of course. but no. seriously no more. i've cut the cord and eaten the placenta.

they said, they said 'the moon'
they said, they said 'the tide'
they lied they lied.
i've cut away, anchor hanked
and now i go seeking silent snow
no no.

I told you I was mad and sometimes find it hard to stay fixed to the point, to the compass point, to the purpose; don't worry about it; let the god lead you; you can always laugh at yourself when you come back, if you come back and if not it scarcely matters.

they told me the rhythm was the purpose
they told me the word was the tune
all my life they told me 'lack'. women lack. alas alack.
bloody toe-rag liars they all were. and now i am the priestess and powerful and pure and free. ha ha.

When the god does not have me in thrall I am quite sceptical about all of this. It seems an odd story to me, and an odd way for a respectable widow lady to carry on.

Once they had real *kore* here, the little girls; pure, skinny, colt-legged, pre-menstrual for the priestesses. But they grew up, they were dark in the shadows, and the priests being both stupid and frightened could not always tell. Suppose, just suppose, their blood had fallen into the pit of the god. Could the world have survived? Contamination. Desecration. Abomination. The blood of the new *parthenos*, the bleeding virgin, is stronger in its vileness than the gods are in their glory. Also, in the mundane, in the quotidian, the god could kill the girls and did. You have to be tough to be a channel of the god. He still kills occasionally – the vapour, the trance, the terror, and afterwards the cool nothing, the deep exhaustion, the void – sometimes still the Pythia does not find the energy to return. But on the whole we are more dispensable and less impressionable. On the whole, we live – less expensive, less wasteful and, somewhere, perhaps, less cruel.

They cannot use the *parthenos*. Of course not. Between bleeding and marrying women are too powerful, too frightening, too bloody dangerous. Shuffle them through – out of their fathers' houses and into their husbands'. Avert your eyes and breathe deeply: they are perilous, these young women. They belong to no man, so they cannot belong to the god. I recall . . . the power of it. My power. You look at a boy, any boy, your own brother who has teased and bullied you for as long as you remember; you look at him, challenging, and he looks away, aside, askance. He knows you have been to the women's shrine: he is not meant to know, but of course he knows. He does not know what goes on there. He does not know and we will not tell him what women carry in our baskets to and from the cave shrine of Athena, the great *parthenos*. You look at him. You don't say anything. You stare straight at him, you stare him down and he does not know if you are bleeding and he is terrified and disgusted and weakened. You laugh. Even your father is uneasy. They are merry months for a girl and she can run out on the hillside in the nighttime. So they marry you off as swiftly as they can and get through the awkward time when you are a woman who belongs to herself as quick and as quiet as possible.

The *gune*, the married women, will not do for the oracle. They belong to their husbands who guard them, and would not lend them even to the god. Especially not to the god, the golden god who rapes and seduces as easily as he sings; a divine lover who might challenge their possession. No way. Married women will not do for the shrine either, since it is not just the god round here who has a taste for rape and seduction – you'd be back to the purity issue before you could say 'fuck me sideways' so to speak.

And mothers are precious and busy and should not be distracted from their duties; should not be raving naked in an ancient temple under a cliff face.

So the priestesses of the shrine of Apollo at Delphi are women who have stopped menstruating; the women who have no name, no word, no status. Fifty years old. They are bloodless, pure like the *kore* and cannot defile anything. They are tough too; they can take it – the ecstasy, the openness and the pantomime that surrounds the real drama of this place. Also more amenable to reason, tamed as the child-woman cannot be and too frightened of the cold not to play along. They are old women dressed up as children in the yellow robes of innocence and death.

They are. We are. I am.

I am the Pythia, the python priestess who can squeeze the life breath out and become a channel, open for use and abuse, by gods and men. I am the voice of the oracle, the priestess of the shrine of Delphi, the pathway of the divine. The god speaks to me, through me, in me and out of me. I am the navel of the world. The omphalos.

The Inquirers come towards evening, struggling up from the coast. There are two reasons why they are encouraged to come in the evening.

Firstly, in Delphi in the evening, the light plays magical tricks. It looks like a place of the gods, like the centre of the world. The river bed is deep and winds serpentine through the gorge, and opens out into the Sacred Plain and the sea of olives moves to its own rhythm like the salt sea down below. The sanctuary rises above the plain and hangs against the cliff side, and the whole is held in silence in the bowl of the mountains. As the sun slips down the sky, the cliff wall glows, red, orange, rose; then mauve, pink, blue; and then suddenly – snfff – the sun sets. The glow vanishes and the enclosing hills turn dun, grey and dead. It cannot fail to impress.

Secondly, hot and tired from the steep climb, weary from the rarefied mountain air, they will drink, and drunk they will talk, and the priests can listen, spy, snoop, watch and so learn the interstices, mappings, plottings, businesses of the world beyond the bay and so calculate a profitable prophecy. When at last they are asleep, the priests come to the House of the *Kore* and we choose the voice, the victim, the messenger, the Pythia for the next day.

If it is I, I will not sleep through the night, but lie on my back and try to smooth out the line between the two confused voices, both of which are true, and prepare myself to go into the place where confusion is too dangerous.

then. dawn. the coming of the dark blue morning. the sun hidden behind the loom of mountain. still cool but heat waiting. hard colours. clear. bright.

The waters of the Kastalian Spring are icy cold. They are icy cold at any time of night or day; but they are coldest purest brightest in the last shards of dark in Delphi at dawn when the priests wake you, when the god awaits you. The Kastalian Spring flows out of its narrow chasm. It is dark in the cleft of the rocks and no one must watch the Pythia as she washes.

so i am washing in the mysterious time between dark and light. liminal time. on the door step between the two worlds.

if i am impure the god will slay me

if i am not open the god will break me

if i am too open the god will destroy me

i am frightened. i hear the holiness of the place, a shiver of air. i know this is the holy place and that the god is waiting. i know the priests have already decided what i will be saying and how much it will cost the Inquirers to learn what it means. i know this. i hold this. and the same time, on the same breath, the god is waiting and i am washing. washing each hair of my head, one by one in the icy cold water. each hair must be cleaned. i am washing away my self. i am emptying myself and becoming as clear as water, clean as water, cold as water, cold as the clear icy water of the Kastalian Spring.

come. they command.

come. they implore.

i breathe deep on my own fear and clean, naked, child-like, i come up out of the cavern.

and we begin.

We process and we sacrifice and we process and we chant and we pray and we sing and we bless and we process. The day grows bright and hot. There is sweat on my lip. As he wipes it away on the white cloth, the priest winks at me; but when he turns and draws the small sacrificial knife I see his hand tremble, just a fraction, over the neck of the cockerel and I know that he too speaks the two languages.

Right up the Sacred Way which coils and undulates between the treasuries: the treasuries of Sykyon, of Siphnos and Magara, of Thebes and Boetia, and past the jewel of Delphi, the treasury of the Athenians with its portico below the great temple itself. All this slow way in the hot sun and I murmur the language of the world. My eyes cling to the cynical smiles of the priest, to the gold buckles of his sandals, and my nose draws on the faint whiff of fine wine on the breath of the acolyte. I think about my pension. I notice that it is getting hotter, that the sun is high now and the shadows black and sharp on the white flag stones. I am amused that the Inquirers are so naive and do not seem to realise that their oracle has been well discussed in priests' house over several days.

Know Yourself is carved on the entrance to the Inner Temple.

I smirk. I know myself. I have nothing to be afraid of. And indeed in this register I am not afraid. Not at all. Not me.

It is suddenly black as we process in to the Inner Temple. Black and cool. We have left the sun outside. We have left the chanting and the singing and the cockerel's blood outside.

Inside as the black disperses it is shadowy cool. It is silent. In the silence I lay my wreath of flowers on the megalith, the omphalos which is almost at the centre. In the dim shade I see the tripod, the three-legged birthing stool that straddles the crack in the rock. A skim thread of smoke emerges, drifting against the shadows of the pillars, which are in fact the pillars themselves, shadowy in the cool dark. I can feel the terror. I can taste the power, like copper in my mouth. I cannot be sick. Not yet.

I step forward. I kneel to the fissure in the rock and the priests and the Inquirers kneel to me. We are all kneeling. I rise. They kneel. I bend forward. I pull the saffron yellow robe over my head and stand naked in front of them.

The two languages clash together. I am the *kore*, the untouched girl child, the one whom the god desires. I am the middle-aged woman with stretched dugs, whose children have gone out from my hearth into their own lives. On the inside of my right thigh, a little above my knee, is a white tangled knot of varicose veins; across my soft and rather protruding belly the stretch-marks slither like snakes. Child. Woman. Girl virgin bride wife mother crone. Both. all. everything. the god calls me.

i am the oracle, the priestess, the pathway.

The priest smiles. I am a vine dresser's widow on to a good thing, with a guaranteed pension and a place in the sun.

either. or. both. and. neither. either. something. nothing. no. thing. all. things. the two languages melt together. pull apart. argue. sing harmoniously. day. night. noise. silence. light. dark. contra. diction.

there. Balanced, capable, present. I am here, here and it is not dark because it is daytime and it is dark in the temple and the god is waiting. and. and for a moment it is possible to keep all this in balance and know that it is all true and all good and that the world is turning under my feet and it is turning me with it and that is real and real is good and then beneath my feet i hear the roaring and a spurt of steam belches out and the god is growing impatient and i leave the sane and step across the line that no one can see and i squat on the tripod and i drop my head on to my chest. they place bitter herbs in my mouth and i chew.

i inhale – snnnnuh

i exhale – aaaaaah.

i draw in the vapour that comes up from the pit, into my nose, into my mouth, into my vagina.

when you squat naked on a birthing tripod and your thighs are forced apart by the sea, and your labia, stretched out, will not cover and hide your vagina and you breathe in the potent magic of the steam which comes out of the bottomless depths of the whole world, then, then you are open, open and broken, open and whole, hole, open to whatever the god will.

the god comes

and there is silence

which of us will speak first?
is there a difference?
we have to go through the wall of silence to find the voice

my silence is in my mouth, with the bitter herbs. my silence is in my womb which does not bleed or breed.

the god does not have body, bones, blood. you have my body. you roar up my vagina and lodge between my navel and my breasts. you come out of your dark slit in the hard rock and into mine, not dry now but soft and sweet. you want a body. you want mine. you will not show me your face. the face of the unbody. do you have fangs? do you want to eat me? do you want to steal my tongue?

how much do you want? how much do you want? it is one thing to be pathway. it is another to be consumed. it is one thing to make space inside me. it is another to let you run amok. to take all my space. to break and smash. you want no conditions and you will not speak for anything less.

BUT YOU ARE HURTING ME

i struggle to love and know that love has no meaning until it is taken beyond the breaking. the way in is the way through and the only way out.

you are carving the road on the nakedness of my skin.

when you ask the gods to speak you cannot tell them what to say.

i want to say, take me. here is a body for you. come out come in. rampage dance sing shout fly. use it. use me.

but i am crushed between

you

sulking under my ribs and in the swelling of my useless belly

and you

anger raging in my head.

i cannot protect you from you. the god who is the father and the god who is the girl child.

the terrain of the great war between the woman child and the almighty father-lover will be a devastation. the fallout will render the whole world desolate, uninhabitable, broken. and that terrain will be my flesh, burned with the falling stars, deafened with the jarring chords of the discordant spheres, crippled with the weight of armies. the war of the giants – red monsters and black monsters and the cutting beat of the centaurs' feet. teeth and flames and the great striped scars of claws.

yes. there will be a great battle and there will be no victory and in the climax not down pushing thrusting and down into the crevasse but uprising whirling – oh graceful flight and consummation and new birth up up upwards and down below the darkness ablaze with light and into some cosmic

hush

shshshshshshhh. shshshshshshsh

a new unity. sweet true flowering. a new creation. no war any more, and a garden of my flowers reclaimed and my body the new and joyful life gestated in silence and birthed in song.

but how do i know i can survive?

and i do not know and i cannot know, because love has no meaning until after the splitting the opening the breaking

and there is a pause and the god withdraws a little and far away, because I have seen it before – for others if not myself – I see tiny and perfect the shadowed temple and the Inquirers standing baffled and impressed and the priests reassuring, their tablets in their hands and the Pythia, who is me, but from here is not me, crouched on her tripod, and her hair stands up on her head and there is spittle on her lips, and snot and sweat on her breasts, and blood and vomit in her fingernails and long scarlet gouges on her flanks

and the god comes again.

now it is the fathers, god the father, who runs a protection racket, the god father, and he loves the good daughter and he hates the bad daughter and i am both and open on the tripod and bloody and sweaty and foamy and snotty i am the bad daughter not the good daughter and the father withdraws his protection.

the father will be angry with the *parthenos* who is his but has broken away to be her own and to run on the hill-side with blood on her thighs. the anger of the father is very dreadful. the good will of the father creates and sustains the daughter, the words of the father created and sustained the universe. if the father is angry it will all go, fall, implode. there will be no light, no matter, no ground, no time, no word, just a grey wind and falling

falling

f

a

l

l

i

n

g

and the centre

O

will not hold

no cord joins the father to the daughter. only the love of the daughter and if the father is angry there will be nothing.

the centre will be blown out. it is called death. it is called madness.

it is called VOID.

this is the anger of the fathers who hold us in being

but the spittle-mad daughter does not die. unnamed but uneaten she is locked in the labyrinth. she wanders there without a thread. she wants to come out. it is too cold and dark. she wants to come out through the fissure, through the rock. she wants to come out with all her filth and her evil mess on her.

the god orders me to kill the girl child.

KILL HER. SILENCE HER INTEMPERATE WAYS.

and what did the *kore* ever do for me, what has she ever done for the widow and the crone, that i should sacrifice myself for her?

i have been her mother

but where is my mother? that is what i need to know. where are the mothers? we need the mothers. i cannot mother the girl child if no one will mother me.

the mothers are treacherous rats. they gnaw through the umbilical cord too soon. the cord is strong and pulsing. it joins the daughter to the mother at the navel. it is the place of inbetween. as i am between the god and the world so the cord is between the mother and the child. the mother rats chew through the cord and there is a hideous gap between blood and air. the mother should wait. the child needs quiet and time, but she is taken and shaken and swung in the cold and the cord is cut.

the mothers. where are the mothers when we need them?

the mothers let us be snatched up too soon. they let us be snatched up into the court of the father; and they rush off into the desert to hide. the mothers are crowned with the stars and the sun and moon are at their feet and they are worshipped, but they are still frightened of the father. they sell the girl child to the father. how will i mother the girl child if no one will mother me?

and i am disintegrating with fury at the mothers, and i am a mother. in the circle of things i am mother and girl child – *kore, parthenos, gune, meter*, priestess – and there is no closure to the circle because i am open. open to the dark pit, my bowels open to scavengers. the god is the scavenger and there is no safe place.

Far away, outside, I can sense that the priests are getting anxious. This is going on for too long and I can still hear, and know that they can hear, my whimpered yells and my enormous whispers. But now the god has me locked, in thrall.

come, sings the god. come inside now, come down come in come into the crack, the narrow way. come.

come in the dark and into the noise and seek for me. you are frightened. you are frightened but you must come. come into the dark place and come to me.

there are no promises. the god does not sing of victory, does not swear that courage will be rewarded, that she who dares wins. first you have to abandon hope, surrender consent, plunge, fall. there may be glory afterwards. perhaps. maybe. or not.

no promises. just come.
come come commmm
language falters, fails in long mmmmmmmmmmm
i resist. i need to resist. i am open. i come.
not too open
not open enough
open

i do not know
mmmmmmmmmmmmmm

Slowly the god leaves me, leaves me. I am cold, cold and heavy and from far away the Temple comes back. I am blinking, filthy, lost, found.

The priest picks me up, holds me warm against him. He carries me safe now against his vestment. 'Shh,' he says tenderly, 'shhh now.' He whispers that I did well, that I am wonderful. I am so tired and held safely. I doze in his arms. He carries me back to the priestesses' house. Lays me on my bed. Calls for someone to bring me a drink, a soft sleepy drink. It is usually like this afterwards. There is the loss, the return. There is the relief, the exhaustion; and then there is the long sleep.

I have laid on a good show, as it happens. They are pleased with me.

The next morning, in another ritual, which I do not attend, the anxious Inquirers are told what the god told me.

If you wish to win your war
You must pay us more and more

Something like that. Something silly. Something that suits the political ambitions of the shrine; something ambivalent, ambiguous, as twisted as the god. But is it what I said? I do not know. I do not know. It is not what I meant to say.

The god comes, comes out of that dark slit in the rock. Comes and possesses his pretended *kore.* The girl child who is really a crafty old woman – fifty years sensible.

If I were really a virgin child, would the god . . .

I do not know.

I do know I am on to a good thing; and so is everyone else here.

I do know that this is Delphi, where the god speaks to us through me.

This is Delphi. The centre of the world. The holy place.

The omphalos.

☾ The shrine of Apollo at Delphi was one of the classical Greeks' most sacred sites: it was believed to stand at the very centre of the world. The oracle there was consulted by all the cities and leaders on both personal and political issues. The shrine became both influential and rich. At the centre of the shrine was a rock crevice, which emitted some sort of sulphurous smoke with intoxicating or hallucinatory properties. A priestess of the shrine – called the Pythia, or Sybil – would crouch over the fissure and deliver the words of the god in a trance-like state (often convulsing, glossolating and howling). The priests then interpreted these ravings, usually into highly ambivalent poems in answer to questions. Although in the most ancient times the priestesses were young virgins, later (probably because of a rape) only women over fifty were used. Some, but not all, of the ritual described in the story is historical. Despite considerable cynicism, Delphi continued to be honoured and consulted into the time of the Roman Empire.

The Greeks divided women carefully into categories by age. *Kore* were pre-menstrual girls. *Parthenoi* (virgins) were young women between puberty and marriage. *Gune* were married women who had not yet had a child and the *Meter* (mothers) were the senior category. Although post-menopausal (and indeed, in terms of contemporary life expectancy, old) the priestesses of Delphi were dressed as *kore*.

Bird Woman Learns to Fly

~

AMONG THE NINETEENTH-CENTURY scholars who turned their minds to the phenomenon of the giant lizard bones, the fossils that were at last emerging into human sight, or rather consciousness, there was a remarkable divergence of opinion. For example:

Samuel Wilberforce believed in neither evolution nor extinction. Richard Owen believed in extinction but not evolution. Jean-Baptiste Lamarck believed in evolution but not extinction. Charles Darwin believed in both evolution and extinction.

The morning after I broke my other wrist Bella came, picked me up from the hospital and drove me home. I knew she would. She is both my best friend and my GP.

(Yes, there are embarrassments in this, but it is one of the consequences of rural life: there is a limited choice in both GPs and friends. Her practice nurse does my smear tests.)

'How did you do it this time?' she asked, after making me coffee and while very sweetly rebuttoning my shirt.

An awkward question. I had done it falling off her son's

motorbike. She was frightened by the motorbike, and, being her, expressed this as disapproval of the motorbike. She would have felt betrayed and looked severe if she knew I had been riding pillion and her fear would have swelled into outright anger if she knew he had had an accident. At the same time she would have felt she had to be nice to me, because the plaster on that wrist was still bright chalk white – unlike the other one which was already a bit grubby. It was time to lie.

'I fell,' I said.

She gave me a look. 'HRT time,' she announced.

'No,' I said.

'Sally,' she sighed, 'Look at me.'

What edges there are in old friendships – what rough terrain and unexpected soak holes. Bella honestly and truly believes, as my doctor, as my friend, as a woman who thinks about these things, and as one who takes them herself, that I ought to take synthetic hormones. Fair enough. But there is something more; over the last couple of years, for the first time in over quarter of a century, she looks better (I mean she has become better looking) than me. She looks terrific, to be honest, fit and vital, her hair luxuriant, her skin glowing and her body warm in the world it inhabits. Whereas it has to be said that I am distinctly frayed, even shabby; and also wrinkling. I look older than she does, although I am not. This is a real change between us. She loves it and I don't blame her. I don't love it. So that affectionate though bossy 'look at me' carries a tiny sharp prick with it, even though we do both look at her with considerable pleasure and satisfaction.

'Why not?' she asked, although we have been here before.

'My curiosity still outweighs my fears.' I smiled a bit to make it sound like a joke.

'Seriously, Sally,' she said. Her eyes narrowed slightly, and she glanced out the window looking for courage somewhere in the herbaceous border. 'Think about your mother.'

There was a pause.

Bella filled it up, 'There is an inherited tendency. There is.'

'I know,' I said. She deserved that.

Lamarck also believed in the inheritance of acquired characteristics. Wilberforce, Owen and Darwin did not.

Did my mother acquire her hump, her brittle bones, her pain, or had they been lurking in her bloodstream, inherited in her genes from conception?

My mother had crumbled. Acute osteoporosis. Little claw-like feet and hands. A hump behind her neck which pushed her feathery chin downwards on to her chest. Pain. Increasing immobility. Dust to dust. Seriously.

I thought about the pictures Bella had made me look at. Slithers of bone, honeycombed, hollowed out, light as air. I had found them beautiful, delicate as lace, as filigree. Lovely and lethal.

I took a breath. I owed it to my mother, to Bella, to myself probably.

'Why don't we do a bone density test?' I offered.

This was dishonest in a way. It would take her time to

get it organised, it would delay the decision or the argument, but it pleased her. I suspect it was better than she had hoped for, all things considered. At the very least she would know that I had done enough reading, or anyway enough listening, to know what I was meant to say.

She withdrew her gaze from the handsome clump of veronica, which appeared to have captured her full attention and smiled. 'I'll get it organised.'

She made me some more coffee, and we sat together in the kitchen until she had to go off to her surgery.

Later Tommy came round. I knew he would. He sidled through the door looking both gawky and sexy in the way that you can when you are eighteen. His hair spiky; his ear stud green glass and glowing; his feet enormous; his hands bony, mobile, intelligent.

He said, 'I told Mum that I'd come and help you with your chores.'

I didn't point out to him the implicit dishonesty in that statement. The fact that he had needed an excuse meant that he had really come for something else.

Somewhere, half way through his first sixth form year, Tommy had 'lost it'. Too much dope and not enough sleep was my verdict; a crunching car accident in a car that he had 'borrowed' from a friend's father (who had, presumably out of loyalty to his son, or to Bella and John or even possibly to Tommy himself – we had all known each other a long time – told the police and insurance company Tommy had been driving with his consent) was Bella's verdict; 'lazy sod' was Ben's verdict, and then, 'Can't you help him, Ma? He's lost it.'

Anyway here he was re-taking his A-levels when everyone else had moved on. Ben, for example, was at this moment somewhere in Peru (according to me enjoying healthy walks in the high Andes; according to Bella being kidnapped by The Shining Path, or murdered by brigands; according to Tommy getting shagged and consuming large quantities of cheap dope). In the meantime, Tommy had become my friend.

To be honest, Tommy had become my toy boy in every sense of that word except that we had not had sex. Not through a shortage of desire. Not on either side. But I was his mother's best friend and he was my son's best friend. There was an inhibition. If either of us would make the first move, would take the responsibility, would openly admit the desire, we might be lovers, but so far we were both waiting, fooling, playing, talking, sub-flirting perhaps; slightly naughty under Bella's benign, innocent and grown-up eye.

He touched my plaster with his fingers. 'I'm sorry,' he said.

He should have been too, even though I had blatantly encouraged him. It had been a wild night; we had taken the bike out in a gap between storm and storm. The wind had dropped, though not very much, and the rain had stopped long enough for the moon to break through the clouds and shine ghostly on the wet roads. It had not been a crash really, neither he nor the bike had been hurt. We had skidded on a corner he was taking a little too fast, and I, dreaming against his hard shoulder, had simply flown free; not far, not dangerously. By the time he had picked me up, assessed the damage and taken me, still on the bike, to the local A & E, the wind was once again driving hard cold rain in from the east, loaded with Scandinavian cold and the dark salt waters of the North Sea. A wild night and I had been excited by the weather, by the bike, by Tommy and even by the strange light sensation I had as I flew from the nest of his pillion to the gravel of the road.

'It's all right,' I said, 'I blatantly encouraged you.'

There was a pause; he looked both shamefaced and enquiring.

'I didn't tell her,' I said. 'I just said I fell.'

His face radiated gratitude. He grinned, self-mocking, young, delightful.

He did my washing-up. I sat and watched him. The older of the two breaks ached dully, deep inside. The new one simply hurt. I tried to tell myself it was the mending that caused the pain, but I was not altogether convinced. I felt old, weary and a bit foolish. Tommy finished putting the china away and came and sat on the hearthrug at my feet. He got out his tin, gave me an investigative look and then rolled us a joint. The dope hit, not hard but strong; definitely more effective than Ibuprofen. I felt chirpier.

After a while he said, 'Shall we go somewhere? Shall we go to the seaside?'

'I'm not sure I can drive,' I raised my fossilised arms.

'I could.'

I could see the glee on his face. I knew what was coming.

The boys are not allowed to drive my car. My car is an E-type Jaguar: older than Tommy and even prettier. It had been Ben's idea. When David died, Ben had been fifteen. About six months later he had said:

'Ma, it's time we had some fun again. There's not a lot of point in Pa leaving all that insurance money if we never spend it.'

We bought him a video camera. I couldn't think of anything for me, but Ben said, 'You need something that makes you look like a glamorous widow. Ideally they should think you killed him for the cash.'

So I got the Jag.

'Will Bella lend you her car?' I asked Tommy, stalling.

'She's gone to the hospital. And Dad's taken his to Newcastle.'

There was a long pause.

'C'mon, Sally,' he said.

'Are you wheedling?' I said.

'"Cutting a wheedle", it's called. Isn't that a great phrase? I read it in *Tom Brown*.'

'*Tom Brown's Schooldays*? What on earth do you know about *Tom Brown*?'

'I found a copy at the church fête. It's cool.' He laughed.

It should not surprise anyone that I made us a picnic and let him drive the Jag. He drove with exquisite caution. I think he was still feeling guilty about the night before.

We went to Dunstanburgh, where John of Gaunt's gaunt ruined castle stands up on its lonely headland and the sea birds wheel and scream on the cliff face below. The storm had blown itself out some time early in the morning, while we were still fussing in the hospital. Although the wind was still slicing in from the sea, lifting spray up over the Caster harbour bar, there was a soft milky light out eastwards and ragged clouds scudding over the broken tower towards the north. The sun was cool and playful, dodging in and out of the clouds, and the air felt alive to the winter and exciting. I walked slowly from the car park along the wide sward path, still feeling slightly delicate and insubstantial. Some of the time Tommy walked with me, and sometimes he slipped his leash as it were and roamed down across the rocky foreshore to the tide line. He threw stones into the water; balanced on larger rocks, jumped over wave splashes, and picked up little treasures to bring me. It was very like walking with Ben and him when they were both little. Except that it was not at all like that. Because – the dope, the painkillers, the shock, last night's excitement, the wild beauty of the day, his sweetness – I was consumed with desire. Each time he came up the beach to bring me some small gift I thought, this time, this time I will say something and he will hesitate and bend his head forward to hear me and I will touch his cheek and . . . I will kiss his mouth and . . . I will lean towards him and he will hold me and . . . and each time I did not. Each exact time was not exactly the right time, although I knew that the place and the day and weather and the hour were all the right time.

Nearer the castle the land begins to rise. There is a small drop between grass and shore; a tiny sand cliff which stretches itself upwards into the rock cliff of the castle promontory itself. Tommy was below this little drop, and suddenly I could not see him. I stood and waited and then after a moment or two walked over. He was immediately below me, crouched and concentrating.

'What is it?' I asked the top of his head.

He looked up at me, his eyes blazing.

'It's alive,' he said. There was a kind of childlike wonder in his voice.

He straightened up, something held tenderly against his chest, and took a couple of steps upwards towards me. The sand drop came almost to his waist and I squatted down, put one hand on his shoulder to balance myself, and held out my other arm. He placed his find on the crook of my elbow, just above the plaster. It was a small black-and-white bird, plump looking, palpitating, bright eyed and too exhausted to move.

'I think it's a Little Auk,' he said. I nodded.

'Is it sick?' his voice rose a note or two, anxious.

'No,' I said, 'storm-wracked. They get blown in from the open sea, if there's a gale. It's exhausted. Sheltering.' I put the tips of the fingers of my other hand on it, and could feel its heart beating very fast against the soft skin inside my elbow. The winter white of its throat and cheeks made even my new plaster look shabby. I held it for a moment. If you hold a small animal or fish in your hand there is substance, weight within it. There was no substance in this little bird.

'It's so light,' I said.

'Birds have hollow bones; sort of honeycombed, filled with air. It's an evolutionary thing. It makes flying easier. They need to be light.'

The bird began to struggle, and I put it down into the

tiny sheltered turf circle that our bodies made between us. It couched there for a minute or so. Tommy touched its head. Then it pushed itself upright, shuffling forward with that awkward old-man gait that auks have. Tommy took my hand off his shoulder balancing me carefully even as he widened the gap between us. The Little Auk lurched out through this triumphal arch, and perched on the very edge of grass. Then, so suddenly that it shocked me off balance, there was a whirring noise, the classical wing beat of the auks, like a wind-up toy, and fast and low over the pebble beach and the broken water's edge it flew – hard, direct, powerful. It was gone.

Tommy hauled himself up the drop, and gave me a hand to get me back on my feet. We looked at each other, stunned, amazed.

'Which came first, do you think: hollow bones or flight?' I asked him.

'*Archaeopteryx* had solid bones, but feathers. They think it could fly. Glide anyway.'

'Bit of luck then.'

'It's all a bit of luck, Sally, you know that. It's random. Random mutation. A mutation for hollow bones wouldn't have been any use, wouldn't have enhanced fitness before flight, would it? Whether you go for top down or ground up – you know, glide or flap theory.'

(Teenagers know the strangest things – this was a boy who had made a dismal balls-up of his A-levels, but could recognise a Little Auk and discourse upon the evolution and causes of flight. To say nothing of driving an E-type Jaguar.)

'Lamarck wouldn't have agreed with you,' I teased him.

'Lamarck? Wasn't he the "inheritance of acquired characteristics" idiot?'

'Yes, but not just. He also believed in evolution by desire. You're a tree-squatting dinosaur; you see some tasty prey on the jungle floor; you think you'd like to be able to glide down and get it. You think it long enough and hard enough and purely enough, and your sweet little nestlings get hollow bones, or feathers or leathery membranes or wings or whatever the next thing is. Lamarck thought that species evolved upwards and upwards until they got arrogant or lazy and then the cycle swung downward again. Little lizards are just lazy dinosaurs. Birds are imaginative, energetic ones.'

He laughed. A good Darwinian. He knew better. I did too really.

We walked on. As the shore fell away below us we kept to the cliff edge, until we came up to the castle itself. Then we turned inland and followed the fence round to the gate. The wind was still hard – cold and bracing, coming straight in from the North Sea. Even so there was an old man standing in the shelter of the ruined wall; and a young woman with a toddler, perhaps three years old. The child was running round in small circles laughing.

Tommy decided to climb up what is left of the tower; there are steps and wooden barriers to stop people falling off. I felt weary now, the walk had been enough without clambering up an irregular spiral staircase. So I told him to go ahead and I sat down on a broken wall and looked out to sea. I was sort of nursing the newly broken wrist against my chest, but the other set of fingers rested on a round lichen-encrusted stone.

I do not think about my mother often. She died just a couple of months before David did, and that second death absorbed all my concentration. It must have been Bella mentioning her that morning, or the grim knowledge that my own bones were thinning out, going hollow and brittle, but the stone reminded me sharply of her humped back against my affectionate fingers. Her woolly cardigan and the lichen both slightly rough to my touch. The stone felt somehow alive, and I recalled clearly the sense of something moving, stirring, deep inside her body, there at my fingertips underneath the ugly lump of pain.

I pushed the grief away and looked around me. The old man was still standing there looking out to sea. Tommy appeared in a window hole above me and when my eye found and caught him, he waved. The woman was trying to help her little boy climb on to a low outcrop of the castle.

Suddenly, piercingly, the child shouted out, 'Don't help me, Mummy, don't hold me.'

Involuntarily I swivelled my face up towards Tommy's window and caught his fierce illuminated glance. Then he disappeared. I knew absolutely that he was running down the stairs and would emerge into the wind with an adult and male demand, with certainty and joy.

I looked out to sea. And then I was light, light and flying.

'I'll make love to him, with him, twice,' I thought. Once for the adventure and once so he knows I really meant it. That's all, only twice.

I thought in a cold clear moment that I had not had sex since David got too ill and I might have lost the knack. And then I was flying. Last night I had not fallen off the bike, but flown. Now I was falling towards him. Falling. Flying. No difference. My bones are light, fine, hollowed, honeycombed, refined by desire. An unbearable lightness of being.

My mother's hump was her desire for wings; they had been folded there, in there, and I had inherited them. She desired them and I acquired them – the wings of her desire, of her lightness, her flight. We evolve, desiring, and then lose our nerves, take synthetic hormones, run away. Her bones were light but her wings stayed folded. Mine are opening now, expanding from my light spine out across my fine collarbones, stretching, not buzzy like auks or bumblebees, but unfolding, opening, huge, soft, strong, like butterflies, like owls.

He comes across the grass eager and stands in front of me. He hesitates, barely, and I smile. He glances around him, notices the woman, the old man, the boy, and he places a hard, grown-up hand on my upper arm. He pulls me towards him, and I am light, almost weightless, flying in to him. Without further ado we slip round, under the castle wall, away from all the eyes, and his hands are so hard and strong, and I see my own hand, magically without the heavy plaster, reach out to touch his face, the clean solid bone of him; and my memory flies too to the memory of my younger hand on my mother's back and feeling the stirring under her skin – little butterfly movements as the chrysalis moves, desires, awakens towards flight. My bones are light and my wings unfold. The plaster, the medical knowledge, and friendship and responsibility should hold me down, but his desire and my desire meet and I am falling and flying. He is part shy, part eager and so am I, but I am flying. Butterfly and dragon, bird and bee. There is no guilt; all of a sudden there is no doubt, no guilt, but only sweetness and lightness.

We are at Dunstanburgh Castle, on top of the cliff, with miles of open coastline stretching north and south. Even as we turn towards the car and escape from the bright enormous exposed spaces it is not clear to either of us if this moment will last long enough. We have to walk to the Jaguar. He has to drive somewhere. My wrists will start aching. We may yet, one or other or both of us, see sense. Or what should pass for sense. We may turn giddy, vertiginous, lose height, come down. But it hardly seems to matter. Now, now his arms hold me and we are flying.

Perhaps we too will be storm-wracked, bone-broken, but I do not care, for I am flying now, hard against the wind itself and my joyful curiosity still outweighs my fear.

Also available from THE MAIA PRESS

IN DENIAL

Anne Redmon

'An intense, sensitive and witty novelist'— Philip Howard, *The Times*

In a London prison a serial offender, Gerry Hythe, is gloating over the death of his one-time prison visitor Harriet Washington. He thinks he is in prison once again because of her. Anne Redmon weaves evidence from the past and present of Gerry's life into a chilling mystery. A novel of great intelligence and subtlety, *In Denial* explores themes which are usually written about in black and white, but here are dealt with in all their true complexity.

£7.99
ISBN 1 904559 01 8

LEAVING IMPRINTS

Henrietta Seredy

'Beautifully written . . . an unusual and memorable novel'— Charles Palliser, author of *The Quincunx*

'At night when I can't sleep I imagine myself on the island.' But Jessica is alone in a flat by a park. She doesn't want to be there – she doesn't have anywhere else to go. As the story moves between present and past, gradually Jessica reveals the truth behind the compelling relationship that has dominated her life. 'With restrained lyricism, *Leaving Imprints* explores a destructive, passionate relationship between two damaged people. Its quiet intensity does indeed leave imprints. I shall not forget this novel'— Sue Gee, author of *The Hours of the Night*

£7.99
ISBN 1 904559 02 6